NOWHERE FAST

Kevin Waltman

SCHOLASTIC INC.

NEW YORK   TORONTO   LONDON   AUCKLAND   SYDNEY

MEXICO CITY   NEW DELHI   HONG KONG   BUENOS AIRES

ISBN-13: 978-0-439-41424-1
ISBN-10: 0-439-41424-5

All rights reserved. Published by PUSH, an imprint of Scholastic Inc., 557 Broadway, New York, NY 10012.

SCHOLASTIC and associated logos are trademarks and/or registered trademarks of Scholastic Inc.

12 11 10 9 8 7 6 5 4 3 2   7 8 9 10 11 12/0

Printed in the U.S.A.   40
First Scholastic/PUSH printing, October 2002

For my parents and my sister.
Thank you for the endless love and support.

Acknowledgments

This is a book about friends—good ones and bad ones. I've been lucky enough to have wonderful friends throughout my life.

First, I'd like to thank all my classmates at Greencastle High School for making my adolescence an enjoyable one.

I'd also like to thank all the friends I've made since—from Indianapolis, Tuscaloosa, Athens, Brooklyn, and all points in between. You've helped me more than you'll ever know. A special thank-you to Brant, Kristin, and Kim for lodging and comfort when I needed it most.

Finally, I want to thank my wonderful and talented editor, David Levithan. Without his guidance and assistance, this book would not have been possible.

Thank you.

Chapter 1

Wilson knows I'm more scared of bailing on him than of whatever threshold we're about to cross. He smiles at me, then turns and strides across the field.

"Wilson," I say. I hiss his name out.

"Let it go, Gary. Enjoy the thrill of it. Don't you feel it?" He says this in his normal, middle-of-the-day tone.

The moon is enormous tonight. It applies a thin gloss to everything, the baby soybean leaves at our feet, the moist soil, the lonely silos' domes. The field stretches another hundred yards toward a sagging fence of corroded wire and a small cluster of trees separating us from the road in front of Roverson's house. Behind us is a county road spotted with telephone wires and a thick stretch of brambles, beneath which we've concealed our bikes.

"Remember," Wilson says, "we both enter on the same side. Don't be an idiot and swing around to the side he can see from his house."

I cup my fingers into the soil and toss some on his back, tell him I'm not that damn stupid. He smiles back at me, taking it as a sign that I'm readying for action.

The air holds a slight residue of the day's heat, like a foul smell lingering well after the source has been eliminated. It makes the night seem pregnant, the full weight of summer ready to unfold. Sweat streams down my chest and stomach. I can feel it pick up speed once it passes my chest, my muscles starting to form into something real, something manlike.

It's the first weekend of summer. The weekend will bring time with Lauryn and with Wilson, and as much time as possible away from my folks. The end of school brings the dawn of our summer jobs: Wilson on a paint crew, me serving scoops at Dairy Castle.

But tonight. Tonight brings us Mr. Roverson's Lincoln.

We're almost to the car when Wilson raises his hand and signals me to stop. The branches give us cover now, low leaves of a tulip tree brushing against the top of my head. I'm only inches behind Wilson, close enough to hear him breathe as he eyes the property, calculating. The heat, Wilson's shallow breaths, the brush of the trees, the hum of insects—it all makes me nervous and pent up.

Finally, after what seems like an hour, Wilson says simply, "Let's go."

We take long, slow strides to avoid crunching the gravel, and soon we're at the big black rusted Lincoln. We both crouch at the passenger's side, and I lean my face against the metal. On the other side, Roverson's house stands dark and undisturbed. I can smell the dust we've raised from the gravel and have to hold back a sneeze.

"Watch for lights, Gary," Wilson instructs. "I'm going in."

He opens the door and enters in one fluid motion. The interior light flashes, its bulb a hot stage light baring us to the world. With a flick of his hand toward the ceiling of the car,

2

Wilson extinguishes it. It was only on for an instant, but it seems to leave an afterglow. I feel as if our every movement remains illuminated, casting shadows all the way back across the soybean field. I fight the urge to turn tail and bolt back to my bike and ride home. Even facing my father on a Friday night seems safer than this.

"There it is," Wilson says. He turns and dangles a lone silver key at me. "Just like Lindy said."

Part of me thought he was bluffing this whole time, that his design on the car was just an elaborate way to get me to admit my fear. But now it's clear his plan is for real. He really did talk to Lindy, and we really are taking this Lincoln for a spin.

Lindy. She was a senior, out of reach for all of us. Now that she's moved from town, that distance is literal. But Wilson has a way of crossing barriers the rest of us can't. Maybe she even gave it up for him, like he said.

I climb in beside Wilson, both of us crouched deep in the car. It feels like an oven, and I wonder how long it's been since Roverson has opened the thing. My shirt is wet with sweat now, sticking to my back.

Wilson explains it to me one more time: He's going to throw it into neutral, then we both crack our doors and get the thing into a slow roll. He won't fire the ignition until we're down the road a bit.

I crack my door and put my foot on the ground, just as lights flood the windshield.

"Down down down," Wilson says. "Get down."

I'm hunched under the dash before he's done talking, my heartbeat banging out cymbal clashes. My thoughts immediately turn to Lauryn. If I get caught in this mess, she'll be done with me for good. It's not even the trouble, the penalties. It's the fact that I've been persuaded by Wilson. Trouble she can tolerate; Wilson's influence she cannot.

Only after those thoughts rush through me do thoughts of my folks enter my head. I can see my mother hanging her head, speechless with disappointment. And I can see my father pacing back and forth in the family room, lecturing, growing louder and more volatile with each passing hour, each empty beer can. I try to squeeze the thoughts off and concentrate on the moment.

The lights begin to thin, washing along the Lincoln as we hear a car roll past. Its tires spray gravel, and a few rocks ricochet against the door with a *ping* only inches from my head. I feel like we're being shot at.

The back windshield absorbs the red of the passing car's taillights for a few seconds, and then it vanishes, crisis averted. I look at Wilson and see his color is gone. He maintains a grin, cocksure and gleaming, but his wide eyes betray the fact that he, too, was scared. It gives me a small satisfaction.

There's no stopping him, though.

"Okay, Gary. Now we roll."

We have to rock the car, timing our thrusts to get it moving. We sound impossibly loud. Finally, it starts to move and Gary peeks his head above the wheel to navigate. We keep pushing it, and I feel us pick up speed, feel the breeze against my bare leg, feel the weight of air against the door. We keep accelerating, and since I haven't lifted my head to see our course, I feel sure there's a tree lurking in front of us or, worse yet, on the passenger side, its trunk positioned to slam the door shut, slicing through the flesh and bone of my leg.

4

"Now?" I ask.

"No."

"Now?"

"Jesus, Gary. Another five seconds."

I can see him squinting into the night.

"Can you see?"

"Keep pushing."

I keep going, each second ticking in a thousand beats of anxiety.

"Now!" Wilson calls.

I jerk my leg in and pull the door shut. Wilson turns the key and the engine roars into the night. He fumbles for a second and finds the lights. They split the darkness to reveal our course—dead straight for a fence.

"Shit," Wilson says. It's not urgent, just a quick obscenity under his breath, like when he hears his name over the loudspeaker in school.

He brakes and turns, the car jolting hard to the left. My shoulder is pinned against the door and my head thuds into the dash. I call out—but not in a whine, I don't want Wilson to think I'm hurt that easy—and hold my head.

"Careful!" I say.

"You okay?"

"I think so. Can you tell? Is it swelling?"

"I can't see it in the dark. We'll check it out once we get down the road a bit. Don't sweat it."

He has the car righted now and winds down the window. He pulls cigarettes from his pocket. He offers one and I take it. He smokes his without touching it, his right hand on the wheel, left arm dangled out to feel the night.

"Where we goin', Wilson?"

"I dunno," he says. He takes the cigarette and ashes it out the window, the ember flying wildly like a miniature firework. It disappears into the blackness. We rush down the county road, a billowing wake of dust behind us, the silence breaking open with the sound of the engine, and I get a powerful feeling—like the engine is echoing, singing our triumph into the country, shaking the woods to life. We make the sleeping world tremor. I feel like we could shatter night itself.

"We can go anywhere we want, I guess," Wilson says.

I met Wilson two summers ago at Kwik Mart, both of us book-in-booking magazines. I was examining a *Playboy* inside a *Sports Illustrated*, he had *Penthouse* in a *Sporting News*. His family was fresh in town, and anything new in Dearborn Springs carries a promise of possibility.

"Put this under your shirt," he said, and handed me a mag.

"And this," he said, presenting a small bag of chips to me.

I did as told and felt my own salt sweating out as we each checked out with just a Coke. My neck was hot, my hands cold, my stomach hollowed as if from a long, violent sickness. But then, after a blurred exchange with the attendant, we were out in the blast of the summer, the heat pulsing down from the sky and up from the pavement.

"Damn fine work, son," Wilson said, and slapped me on the back.

We walked a few blocks to the train tracks and sat down to inspect our loot. We didn't find much to say—I was even worse

6

in conversation then than now—but he kept smiling at me. Smiling like he knew something. That seemed just about right to me.

We split the chips and flipped through the magazines. He already talked about girls like he had experience, and I tried to absorb all I could. I'd been sneaking peeks at nudie mags for a year already, but this was the first time it seemed okay. With Wilson guiding, turning pages, laughing at the jokes and stories, it didn't feel like a dirty secret anymore. It felt normal.

Wilson is a few months older, but it's always seemed like years. He has a brother, Matt, at college. I've met Matt only a few times and suspect a decent share of Wilson's knowledge is borrowed from him.

We rose to go home, and I explained that I couldn't take the magazines with me. I was sure to get caught.

"Don't sweat it, Gary," he laughed. "I'll hold onto them for you. Meet me here Thursday after lunch and we'll go get a few more. We'll even find a place for you to stash some at home."

It's been that simple ever since. *Show me where your pops keeps his beer*, he says; I show.

Drink this; I drink.

Smoke this; I smoke.

He has always known where to get things, too. He knows where the parties are—it used to be all those lame middle-school parties where kids were afraid to talk to one another, but now they're real parties, high-schoolers with kegs, dropouts with their own place, haphazard gatherings deep in the country with warm beer and low-quality hash. He knows who can buy. He knows who's doing who. He knows how to get action with girls. And, most important, he knows how to get me to play along: All

7

he has to do is hit me with that smile and lend me some of his strength.

So when he said he knew where to get a car, I shouldn't have been surprised.

"Roverson's," he said.

"Mr. Roverson?"

"Hell, yeah, who you think? Guy never leaves the house now, and I know for a fact he's got a spare set of keys in the glove compartment."

"You mean we're taking his car?"

"Jesus, Gary. Of course that's what I mean. He doesn't even open his blinds. He ain't gonna miss it. We're gonna swipe that sonofabitch and take a ride." He said it all with a flourish, a dreamy lilt to his voice—falling in love with his own scheme.

There was no sense in challenging him. When Wilson gets that tone, it's like trying to stop the wind from blowing.

In the end, we don't go much of anywhere. It's not the first time either of us have been behind a wheel—if there's one thing our fathers have been good for, it's been taking us out for practice drives—so driving pales in comparison to the thrill of the take.

We raise dust on back roads for a good hour and a half before Wilson decides it's time to go into town. We gas up. We pull into the parking lot of the supermarket and watch the older kids drag back and forth, windows down, looking for anything to change the sameness of this strip.

The whole time I feel certain we're going to be caught. I'm just waiting for a hand to come to rest on my shoulder, squeezing as a voice says, *We got a call in on a Lincoln, boys. You wouldn't happen to know anything about that would you?*

But it doesn't happen. Even in Dearborn Springs, Indiana, the cops must have better things to do than track down fifteen-year-olds on a joyride.

Amber pulls up beside us. She gets out and leans against her daddy's Thunderbird, and through the windows I can see her cleavage. I try not to stare. I try not to think about all those things Lauryn won't let me do.

"Wilson England and Gary Keeling. Who's driving you two kids around?"

"I got the wheel," Wilson answers.

"You got your license, Wilson? I didn't know that."

"Got no license," he says. "Just got the wheel."

He's good. He talks a fine game and has the guts to back it up. Every girl our age or younger is scared to death of him, but he was getting busy with older girls last summer. That, of course, just gave him more confidence. It shines on him like a crown.

Amber walks around her car to us, smiling. Wilson always tells me I should get with Amber. *She's a good starting point*, he'll say. She gets closer and wrinkles her brow.

"That car," she says.

"It's my uncle's. He's spending the summer in California."

Amber stares at it for a few more seconds until the suspicion drains from her face. Wilson is the best liar I've ever known. He has the knack for making his words seem like the most fundamental truths in the world. *It's my uncle's* sounds as obvious as *The stars are out* if Wilson wants it to be so.

Amber decides to ride with us for a while. We go all the way

9

to Cloverdale, where we can use her fake ID to get a couple of six-packs. In exchange for her contribution to our delinquency, Wilson lets her have the wheel, and she takes us back out into the country, deeper than before. She drives all the way to Pine Hill Cemetery, where we park.

On my second beer, I can already start to feel the buzz sink in. I rub my head where I hit it against the dash. I think I can feel a bump, but Wilson and Amber assure me there's nothing there.

"Toughen up, kid," he says, trying to embarrass me.

Wilson keeps us plied with smokes, and we talk about the town, the summer, the classes she's already had that Wilson and I will have next year.

The thrill of the theft has worn off, and the alcohol is taking me in the wrong direction. *This is it*, I think. *This is summer in Dearborn Springs. Meandering through the country, scamming beer, having these same conversations, only updated by a year. None of it ever changes.* I'm sitting up on the hood of the Lincoln, Wilson and Amber on the ground at the driver's side. I take another drink and look down, see him pushing his hand up against her chest. That will not change, either.

Everything is always the same here.

They talk low to each other. When they laugh I wonder if it's about me. Finally, Wilson remembers I'm here. "When we head back in," he says, "I think we should let Gary drive."

"Shoot," Amber says. "You're kidding. Gary's way too good for that. No way will he drive after a few beers."

"Don't shortchange my boy. Just 'cause you don't see him in detention doesn't mean he's not crazy. Kid helped me lift this car."

10

"Wilson," I say. I try not to shout it, but it comes out like a guilty squeal.

"You said this was your uncle's."

"It is."

Again she buys the lie. I can see it in her confused face.

"I have no problem," Wilson explains, "stealing from family. No more than I do from anybody else."

It takes a second, but Amber catches on. Then she looks up at me approvingly. Winks.

"They'll send you to juvey. You'll miss your sophomore year."

When she says it, I can tell she's impressed. Wilson has criminal ambitions usually reserved only for juniors or seniors. I feel a small jolt of pride at my own role in his doings, and I take another drink.

We're parked in the turnabout in the cemetery, the only way out leading down the hill. The cemetery is quiet, sparse pines looming over the tombstones. To the north, the plot ebbs into thick woods, and we can hear life rustling in them. To the south, it slopes sharply for a hundred feet, where the hill levels. We can see cars, their lights weaving in blurs, coming from miles away. When they get close, the three of us start to tense, ready to hide the beer and split. But each time they turn off, going their lonely way.

Wilson breaks the silence.

"Hell. I might miss my sophomore year, anyway."

I look at him and wonder what story he's crafting now.

"My pops might get relocated. He works down at Dana. He said they're negotiating a move to Pennsylvania. I guess there's still a chance they'll stay here, but we won't know until later this summer."

I look at Wilson to see if he'll betray his lie, but he just returns my stare—he's telling the truth. This is news to me, and it hurts. I try not to let my reaction show, but it lowers me. Wilson is my best friend and, it sometimes seems, my only one. Lauryn is a friend, too, but it's not the same. Before pairing up with Wilson, I would kill time alone, playing on my computer, riding my bike aimlessly, watching sports with my dad if he was in a decent mood. I wasn't outcast or bullied, but I was usually alone.

"I didn't know your dad worked there," Amber says. "Mine does, too. But he said he'd find another job here before he dragged us all across the country."

"Not mine," Wilson says. "Hell. He moved us all over the place before we landed here. He won't think twice about yanking us up again."

I walk away from the car and sit at the edge of the cemetery, smoking in silence. The boil has finally left the air, and the breeze feels cool against my shoulders. Wilson comes and kneels in front of me, the earth plummeting behind him, so that he is outlined only by the dark horizon of sky. Last summer at the rock quarry he did a similar thing, knelt in front of me at the edge. Then, like a bird hopping from its perch, he gave a quick jump off the side. He landed safely on a shelf of rock only two feet below, but it was enough to give me the jarring shock he was seeking. I feel like he might try something like that again—something crazy to scare me—but if he does, this time I don't think I'll recover. Not now.

Instead he feigns a punch to my jaw. His fists are big, like they belong on a man twice his age.

"What up, Gary? Why you off here sulking?"

"I shouldn't be here."

He looks over my shoulder to where Amber is sitting. "Her? Gary, that's nothing. You want her? I can arrange that. I'm telling you, boy, she is not a picky girl."

"It's not that," I say, which seems like a lie even though it isn't. "I just don't feel like I belong here."

"Fuck it, then. Let's go."

He stands and walks to the car, tells Amber to get up, we're heading back to town.

But none of that, not his willingness to change the course of the night for me, not his grant of permission for me to drive, not his suggestion for Amber to ride up front with me, not the glimmer of power I get as I swing the Lincoln back into the parking lot next to her car—none of it can make things right.

Only later—when we're edging the car along the gravel in front of Roverson's and then sprinting across the field to our bikes, hastened by the wild barks of country dogs awake with our scent—only then do I feel whole. Only seeing Wilson lead the way to escape, my heart drumming with fear and the adrenaline that attends it, do I feel like I belong to anything at all.

Chapter 2

The last thing I want to do the next morning is wake him, but all it takes is for me to turn on the tap. I hear him rumble on the couch.

"Goddamn. Shut that racket off, kid."

I click the tap off and stand still, hoping he'll go back to sleep. I'm going to Lauryn's to watch a movie. It's easy boyfriend material: Sit there on the couch, hold her hand, and act interested in the flick. Still, she'll know if I'm upset. She always knows. Even yesterday there was something off about her, like she suspected me, and I wonder if she somehow knows about the car.

I try to put this out of my mind, to calm down. I drink my water.

"I can hear you, Gary. I can hear you drinking. For Chrissakes, get out or go upstairs. You know Sundays I need my rest."

I know he needs his rest on Sunday mornings. I know he likes to get loaded on Saturday nights, even more than other nights. I know it's not a good idea to disturb either of those efforts.

It's too late, though. He's up.

"Christ, Gary. A man asks for simple pleasures and you gotta go fuck it up."

"It's almost eleven," I say. Bad move.

He pushes on either side of my collar with his thumb and index finger, and I bend back against the counter. I come up to his chin now, and if I wanted I could resist his push. Conditioning for basketball didn't earn me much playing time, but I can feel my body gaining strength.

"I can read the goddamn clock, Gary."

He flings the refrigerator door open and stares into it. The shades are drawn, and the refrigerator light fills the room obscenely. It puts his body in a silhouette that does him no favors. He is one of those men who, moving through the day, still looks strong and almost young: the man who made second team all-state in football, who walked on at Purdue. In old pictures, I can see why my mom fell, and I still remember him hoisting me atop his shoulders with ease even when I was six, seven, eight years old.

But the current outline of his body doesn't lie. He's getting fat. Too many cheeseburgers. Too many tenderloins. Too much alcohol. He does everything too much.

"Where the hell is your mother?" he asks.

"She was going to the store, then church."

He grunts. He leaves the fridge open and walks to the sink, turns the tap on full blast. He splashes water on his face and dries it on the hand towel. He digs in his pockets, looking for a cigarette, sees them on the counter and shakes one loose, lights it. Then he walks back to the fridge and stares again.

"What's she getting?"

"I don't know. Can't read her mind. Why don't you call her on your cell phone and ask?" This is a good dig. He broke his cell phone two weeks ago when he threw it across the kitchen in response to a call he received. As soon as it's out of my mouth, though, I know it's a mistake. What makes me do it? What makes me dig at him these days even though I know silence is the best option?

He stalks across the kitchen toward me, but I refuse to flinch. He cuffs me under the chin, like a bear toying with prey. "You're a smart little turd this morning, huh? I'll shut that tongue right up."

He is all threat and intimidation. He's never hit me with a closed fist, and I've never seen him do it to my mom. He is pushes and bumps and jerked arms and slaps on the back of the head.

He walks back to the couch and turns on the TV to a low drone. There is nothing on but news shows, and he mutters his disapproval at the set—"fucking junk."

He pulls the blanket around his bare shoulders.

"Why you up so early?" he asks.

"I'm going over to Lauryn's. Watch a movie."

"Not likely."

I begin to stammer out a protest.

"Shut it. Call her and tell her you have chores."

"But I don't."

"If you make me get off this couch again you will hate your own life. Call her."

I go to the phone and pretend to call. When he falls back asleep against the murmur of the television, I make a quiet exit. I don't care if there will be hell to pay later. Later won't be any different than now.

* * *

16

When I get to Lauryn's she is upset because I'm late. No, not upset. But she mentions it. I explain about my father, and she lets it go. She apologizes and says she was afraid I'd spent the night at Wilson's. She kisses me on the cheek to make up, and all is well.

The house is empty.

"Where're your folks?"

"My mom's in Terre Haute. She needed to go to the mall. My dad went down to the office."

I feel a quick leap in my chest. I begin to catalog all the possibilities of having Lauryn alone in her house for an entire morning. The feeling goes straight to my crotch and I sit down fast so Lauryn won't see. She senses my mood right away, though.

"We're going to watch a movie, Gary. I rented this movie just so we could watch it together. And since you spent the entire weekend until today with Wilson, it's overdue. So it's the movie. Don't get frisky just because my parents are gone."

I manage to say something that passes for understanding, but inside I feel a drop of disappointment. The drops keep welling up with her, and soon I'll have an ocean of unused lust inside me. I don't know what will happen then, when the weight of it shifts the scales from patience to desperation.

I don't even tell her that I don't want to watch the movie, that Wilson and I stole into the theater to watch it and it seemed just like any other movie.

She smiles at me. "You've never been too pushy with me," she says. "I like that about you."

Her skin looks soft and wet, like she's come straight from the shower. The overhead light raises the soft highlight of her

17

cheekbones and forehead against the rest of her mahogany face. She keeps her hair short, shorter than mine—a sexy little fuzz that she calls her "summer 'do." Her oversized T-shirt can't hide the fact that she is curving into a new body. I eye all this and wonder how it came to be that I've never been too pushy with her. Something has to happen with her this summer.

Things were a struggle with Lauryn from the start, but not as much as they are now. I'd seen her in school a bunch, but we had different classes and barely spoke—just nods and an occasional "Hi there" in the hall.

When we finally did have a conversation last summer at the pool, I didn't exactly give the best impression. Wilson and I had been terrorizing younger swimmers at the local pool with cannonballs off the board, until the lifeguard had to shout us down, threaten us with permanent expulsion—not that Wilson and I went there much, anyway. We were both still laughing at our antics, our voices echoing off the wet concrete around the pool. I plopped down in a chair to bask in the day, content, while Wilson went to the concession stand for drinks.

"How mature," the person next to me said. I looked over and it was Lauryn, and all I could tell in the glare of the sun was that she was frowning at me.

"Hey, look. We're just having fun. Lighten up."

"Well, your 'fun' ruined my book." She held up a soggy copy of *Animal Farm*, one of the few books I'd actually read for class in middle school. I liked the book, even if I did have to take a ribbing from Wilson when I talked about it in class.

I apologized and offered to give her my copy.

"You read?" she asked. "A guy that hangs out with Wilson England dares to open a book?"

"Well, I read that book."

"Oh, yeah? Did you get the allegory?"

It stumped me. I remembered the teacher mentioning something about this in class, but it seemed unimportant at the time. I really did feel bad about messing up Lauryn's book, though, and her smug tone made me nervous. I wanted to say something intelligent. But "Look, I just liked the part where the animals throw out the master" was all I could come up with.

Lauryn thought this was endlessly funny, and it seemed to soften her demeanor toward me. By the time Wilson came back with Cokes, I'd already set up a time to come over to her house with my copy. I didn't think of it as a date, even though when I told Wilson later, all he could keep saying was "You're *in!*"

We started just as friends, though—watching movies together, talking on the phone, confiding in each other about our frustrations in Dearborn Springs. It took me most of the summer just to work up the courage to try to kiss Lauryn, but when I did everything seemed perfect, like I was finally accepted completely.

"I've been hoping you'd do that," she said after I kissed her.

"I didn't know if you wanted me to," I said.

She looked down at the floor, said that she did. But she said she figured most of the boys in town would never even consider going out with her.

"I'm different," she said. "I'm just some Goody Two-shoes to them. And, well, I'm . . ." She ran her hands along her arms, pointing at her skin.

"They're crazy," I said. "Don't worry about them."
It was that slow, that simple.

Now Lauryn pops in the movie and lets me hold her hand. We sit upright, rigid. It's as if instead of watching a flick at my girlfriend's, I'm spending Sunday morning like my mother would prefer: sitting at attention in a pew.

The movie is fine, but I can't stay focused. I keep looking at her instead of the screen. And instead of the dialogue, I hear her breaths, the drip of the bathroom faucet, or the lazy wheeze of cars outside.

After an hour of this, I'm lost completely. I consider what the schools tell us about drugs and alcohol, about how they kill our brain cells and thieve our attentions. Last month my guidance counselor called my mom in, explained that my teachers were concerned over my lack of participation in class.

The counselor kept explaining things. I might have good attendance, but I am the most mentally absent child in the class. And while my grades are decent, it is because of natural talent, not effort or focus. I'm not living up to my scores on aptitude tests. It is reason for concern among all parties.

Aptitude. That's a curse growing up in Dearborn Springs.

I watched my mom's brow furrow as the meeting lengthened into the early evening. The counselor spoke of behavioral traits, mood swings, and my inability to communicate with other students. By the end, my mother had a sick look of resignation, her face the color and texture of wet chalk.

On the ride home she pressed the brakes, like I might pay closer attention at a slower speed, like the gravity of the brakes might squeeze the truth from me.

"Have you ever smoked marijuana, Gary?"

"No." I answered quick and huffy, acting insulted by the question.

"Have you ever been offered drugs? You can tell me. From Wilson? Does he take drugs? What about upperclassmen?"

"Mo-om," I said, trying to answer all her questions at once.

That was the end of the conversation. And with summer beginning, school became as trivial to her as it is to me. Besides, she has other things to worry about.

My mind retraces all this while the images flash on the screen, and when it stops racing I feel like I'm landing, dropping down on the couch beside Lauryn like some meteor hurtling through the atmosphere. I feel surprised to be there. Surprised that the movie is still going. Surprised that Lauryn's hand is in mine.

"What's wrong?" she asks.

"Nothing." I rub my thumb along her index finger, trying to soothe her. I look down and see myself do it, all my attention there. My fingers are changing. The knuckles are bigger, and the skin is rougher. I am growing out of my hands.

The balance of my skin against Lauryn's intrigues me, and I wonder again how much damage I'm doing to my brain if I'm fascinated by observing my thumb run against the swirls of print on Lauryn's finger.

"You seem far away sometimes," she says.

"No. I'm right here." I kiss her on the cheek and then reach my hand under her chin to turn her toward me. She lets me steal a little kiss on the lips. I take it and decide not to press for more until after the movie.

When the movie's done, and when she's knocked my hands away from her chest, we sit there in silence. Neither one of us is angry, but there's a slight charge in the air, like the next word might set something off.

"Wilson might move," I say.

She blinks at me. I know she takes this as good news but won't admit it.

"His dad's company might move," I continue.

"I know. I heard my parents talking about it. That would mean a lot of people might be moving then. I know Mary's dad works there. And Chuck's. And Amber's."

She gives me a leer when she says Amber's name, and I feel guilty for things I haven't even done with Amber. Things I've barely even thought about. I could tell her that Amber won't move either way, but I don't want to feed Lauryn's mistrust.

"Why don't I know these things? Why am I the last to find out?"

"Because you don't pay attention, boy. Your head is always in some place apart from your body. And you don't eavesdrop on people and meddle — not like everybody else. Which is nice. That's part of the reason I like you. You're my daydream boy. But that's also why you don't know something everybody else in town is talking about."

She's right. I try to latch onto the compliment of what she said. Then I kiss her and we go in search of another daydream.

We find this one in her pop's record collection. Mr. Avery's

22

albums line the shelves of his den, and we sort through them, amazed at the intricate cover art and the substance of the records themselves. Vinyl—it seems like we're in a museum. I love going through his records. There are hundreds of them—soul music mostly. It's attached to some other time when soul meant something else. Something as foreign to my life as possible.

I don't dare tell Lauryn this, though. I don't say anything to acknowledge that her father is black and her mother is a mix of several races—and that whatever that makes her, it is a long way from my white skin. Only once did I broach the subject of our races, and she sulked for a week. She wouldn't talk to me except to say that I must think she's some kind of trophy, a way to prove something to the rest of the town. Since then, my words to her have remained absent of color.

We lie back in the deep carpet and listen to the music. It's not that I like the music that much—there's nothing in it for me—but it is a way to crawl inside her, to feel a part of her pulse. The sun fills the room, and we can see dust and carpet fibers dancing in the rays above us. She lets me touch and kiss her, my lips on her neck, my fingers on her belly, and I'm careful not to let any part of me stray too far to upset this balance. The stereo pops and hisses between songs, the sounds that go with the sparks our fingers give each other.

Then Mr. Avery comes home. We hurry the records back into their sleeves, even though he doesn't care that we listen to them. We give the breathless appearance of kids caught in the act, even though we were only kissing.

He calls us out to the kitchen, and we sit with him. He talks to me like an adult. Asks me about studies, about my summer job, about music and sports. He seems more interested in my life than I am.

Lauryn sits there quietly. She gets up to fix herself some iced tea, extends an offer of the same to us, and then sips and watches us talk.

I hate this part of it. There's something in me that resents Mr. Avery for being nice to me, like he's robbing me of some vague pleasure. Yes. That's it. I want to be the dangerous boyfriend the disapproving parents frown on. I want him slanted against me, Lauryn and me united in our defiance against his rule.

But that's not how it is. He is genuinely kind to me and I—for the most part—am a genuinely good boyfriend to Lauryn.

It's too perfect, though. I know I can't live up to his expectations.

Chapter 3

I'm out with Wilson again, making our approach on the Lincoln again. This is our third time now, and the thrill of theft is beginning to wear off. Our edge is softened even more by the beers we drank before we came.

We cross the gravel road, our stealthy creep replaced by a swagger. My feet feel several inches off the ground. But inside me there is a gnawing disturbance, like something rotten churning toward shore. Wilson has talked all night about moving to Pennsylvania but won't indicate whether it's a definite thing or not. If he's not talking that up he's been silent and moody. He bristles, his normal mischievousness replaced by a smoldering violence. I hate it when he's this way.

We have the car rolling, and Wilson fires it up earlier than usual. Our carelessness generates a sense of danger, like we need to flirt with getting caught to make it more fun. Still, it doesn't quite work. We can't replicate the feel of the first theft. And whatever fun there is to it burns up in Wilson's hot silence.

"Where we gonna go tonight?" I ask.

No answer.

"You wanna go into town?"

Nothing.

"We could go to Cloverdale and get a six-pack."

Still nothing from Wilson. He drives a few miles, our headlights slicing through wisps of fog. The road seems filled with pitfalls. I keep looking to the edges for eyes of animals about to bolt for the road. Dogs, raccoons, fox, deer. All of them pose danger in my mind. Nothing happens, though. Nothing happens here even when I feel a change, a rupture, imminent. Nothing.

Finally, Wilson says, "Why the hell don't we go to Indianapolis?"

I don't dare disagree with him. Normally, a trip to the city would seem a thrill, as exciting as anything Wilson could suggest. But his mood taints the idea and makes it feel more like a threat than an option.

He was like this when I first saw him get in a fight. It was in school last year, and he snapped on Merle Fuller, a big farm kid who always stank of manure. Nobody messed with Merle, mainly because of his size, but also because he kept to himself, enduring his intermittent and subdued attendance until he could stay home legally. He may have been rough, but he wasn't one to cause distress.

Wilson had been grumpy all day. In first period, he'd misbehaved and prodded Mrs. Emtman until she could no longer ignore him: She gave him detention, and he just grew murkier.

When we were at our lockers, I asked him what was wrong. He refused to answer—later he would say that Stephany, a junior, had declined to go out with him that weekend, but that didn't seem like enough; he never got worked up over girls. I decided to let it go.

I had my books in hand and was headed to class when I

26

heard the first thud of Merle dropping to the floor. More thuds came as Wilson jumped on top of him, knees on his chest, elbows, forearms, and fists crashing down.

When it was finished Merle was bloody and crying, a bewildered confusion owning his face. Wilson was quiet and cool, huffing out the last of his rage. He explained to me and to the teachers and counselors that he'd hit Merle to defend Lauryn and me.

He said, "Why does your buddy go out with that little nigger girl?" And then I had no choice but to hit him after that. That was Wilson's story and he never wavered from it. It was plausible. Not just from Merle, but from half the kids in our school. So I never openly questioned him. I never entirely believed him, either. It took an entire week for things to get back to normal between us.

He's got that same edge to him tonight. He has all the potential of a lit fuse.

We're on the highway, streaking west toward the city. Wilson rips past semis like a train past a closed depot. He cuts in front of them without using his blinker, drawing their brights.

Wilson extends his middle finger to them and says, "Have a nice night, loser."

"What's the problem, Wilson?" He's pushing eighty-five and I can't pretend not to notice anymore.

"No problem, Gary. Why you so antsy?"

"Look. We don't have to go to Indy on my account. I'd be happy going back into town and getting more beer."

"We're *not* going to Indy on *your* account."

He raises the radio volume. It's the classic rock station, and it blasts Van Halen between bursts of static. Bugs die *flit flit flit* on our windshield. Wilson flicks the wipers to knock them away, the blade dragging dryly across the glass. I can't take this. I can't take a whole summer of Wilson this way, pushing against me stubbornly, mutely, dissolving into the monotonous ache of life in Dearborn Springs instead of breaking that pattern, making things happen. That's why I stick to Wilson in the first place.

The ride lasts for forty-five minutes before that rhythm is shattered, before Wilson breaks up this sameness.

We're nearing the city, close enough to see the lights glowing in the shallow sky, when it happens. I'm slow to notice it, the beer retarding everything for me. But when Wilson snaps to attention behind the wheel, springing out of his slouch into a rigid alertness, I know something is up. It's only then that I see the rolling lights playing tricks across our dash, the inside of the Lincoln beginning to swirl in red and blue. I wonder how long they have been there, how long I've been in this half-awake state while they've been in pursuit.

When I turn around I can see there's still a sizable gap, but I can't tell if the police car is gaining or not.

"How fast were you going, Wilson?"

"I dunno. Not as fast as I am now."

There are no other cars between us, and in front there are only a few far-off semis lumbering with their cargo. Their lights flash against the orange-and-white barrels that narrow the highway from three lanes to two. Beyond them I can see heavier traffic near the downtown exits, but I feel like the landscape is helplessly barren, and we are doomed and exposed.

"Jesus, Wilson. You're not going to pull over?"

"Gary, you remember an hour ago when we crept into this

car and lifted the key from the glove compartment? That makes this a stolen car. You do realize that, don't you?"

"We're busted, though. This is only gonna make it worse."

"If we can get up to that traffic in front of us, we can hit an exit and they won't see us."

My breath goes short, and I feel dizzy with what he's telling me. I look at the speedometer and see it quivering at ninety-five.

"Wilson! Stop! Stop! There's no way to get out of this. You're gonna get us killed."

He looks over at me, not breaking the car's momentum. He relaxes his pose, his shoulders dropping. He moves his right hand from the wheel and curls his left hand over it, guiding the car with his wrist.

"Gary," he says, condescending. "Gary. How many times are you going to try to talk me out of things? Sometimes we have to try even when we know we can't win. Even when everything is stacked against us. Otherwise, what's the point of doing any-thing?"

He slaps my knee with the back of his hand and laughs. He flashes his teeth at me and then stares back to the road ahead of him, his left index finger pointing the way.

"So just hang on," he says. "We're gonna head for that traffic up there. That cop catches us before we make it, we are two screwed individuals. I mean, we are fucked. And that might happen. But I want to try like hell before that happens. You with me?"

I look again behind us and see the police have cut into our ground. My palms start to sweat. In front of us, though, I can see we've narrowed our distance to the traffic considerably. In a flash of adrenaline I feel like there's a chance.

"Go go go," I say.

Wilson hits whatever's left on the accelerator, and the Lincoln gives a throaty roar and jump. Without looking at the dash I know that we've broken a hundred. I keep checking the mirror against my will and each time I see the police a bit closer, close enough now to hear the siren. Still, we're gaining on the trucks faster than the cop is gaining on us, and soon I can make out the designs on their mud flaps.

The Lincoln handles the speed well, no rattling or shaking. Only the engine seems bothered by it, its pitch rising into a high whistle. Wilson keeps it floored until we're close enough to the truck to see the tire treads. Then he swings around it in one smooth arc. When we clear the truck and get back in the right lane we see a smattering of traffic in front of us, but it doesn't seem like enough to get ourselves lost in.

I look back and see the lights of the cop car begin to split the darkness around the truck.

Wilson cuts our headlights and we go hurtling into a darkness relieved only by the other lights along the highway, the traffic headed the other way, the still distant sparkle of the city.

"Wilson!" I scream. "Turn the lights back on before we get killed."

"I don't want him to read our plates."

"What the hell does it matter? It's not our car."

Wilson drives in silence for a bit, racing ahead. As he does, I think that now is not the time to question his judgment, that I should just let him do whatever he wants at this point.

Finally, he answers.

"Look. We still have to get back to Dearborn Springs. If they call these plates in, there's no way we get within two counties of home without getting busted in this thing."

I try to stammer out a protest, but I know I'm at Wilson's mercy. I have no choice in this matter; all I can do is hold on.

Wilson races toward the rear of another truck and swings around it, but a Honda is in the left lane, hovering just in front of the semi. We edge toward it until I'm sure we'll hit its bumper. Then Wilson jerks us back into the right lane, earning a deep honk as we cut off the truck. In front of us is another car, a big red boat of a Chrysler, and again we ride its tail close enough to be its hitch.

Beside us, the passenger in the Honda is gesturing at us frantically and I can see his lips issuing obscenities. The truck, angrily tailgating, flashes its brights and gives us another honk—the highway version of lightning and thunder.

Our speed has decreased, but Wilson alternates between hitting the gas and riding the brakes. The jerks of the car increase the feeling of volatility. Every second feels like the last one before we wind up in a giant twist of bent metal and bits of glass.

I can smell the heat rising from the engine and the tires. There is the stench of rubber in flame, but it has a sweet edge to it like there is honey in the night air. I clicked the radio off long ago, and now the car is filled with the screeches of brakes and the hum of tire on road. But that is not the only thing humming—Wilson is humming, too. Some artless, meandering tune. But he is humming nonetheless, as if we were cozying along a country lane, winding next to some stream, poles in hand, searching for the best place to get out and cast for bluegill.

I am both inspired and frightened by his appearance of calm.

Boxed in by the three vehicles, I figure we're caught. The police car is almost perfectly diagonal from us, gaining in the left lane on the Honda, giving those riders the same treatment the truck is giving us. They have nowhere to go, though. They can't come into our lane without hitting us, and construction barrels whisk by in a blur on their left.

I'm about to plead with Wilson again to give up, to surrender before somebody gets killed, but before I can he screams at me: "Hold on, son! Here we go now!"

We pass an exit and he jerks the wheel to the right so fast I'm surprised our back end doesn't wrap around the sign. We immediately start bumping over the uneven shoulder, the speed shaking us like we're caught in an agitator. We start to edge around the Chrysler, our hood nosing past its back bumper. We're only about a hundred yards from the exit, and I understand Wilson's plan for the first time. In front of us, the Chrysler, unaware of our location, starts to edge right as if it might exit. Wilson jumps on the horn like a madman—screaming, too—and with enough volume that I actually think he wills the Chrysler back to the left.

That clears the way for us to exit. As we speed onto the ramp, I look back to see if the cops made it over. They didn't. I see them crossing the median to take the opposite exit, but I know by the time they do we'll be long gone.

Wilson pops the lights back on when we hit the base of the exit, merging quickly.

"Look for a place to hide this thing," he says.

We don't get more than a block when I see a promising spot: an open space next to a van in the drive in front of a house.

"There," I say. "Pull in on the other side of that van."

Wilson does it and we wait. We get out of the car and crouch by the van. From there we can see the street, and we're already on foot in case we need to bolt.

Finally, we see the police car go past. We creep to the edge of the street so we can watch it roll away, mix with the wash of traffic. I look the other direction and see that we are only blocks from downtown, the skyline thrust dryly into the boiling night. All around us the city is alive with the weekend. Normally, its bustle makes me feel insignificant. But tonight I feel superb. I feel like we've ripped the carpet from beneath the entire city, pulled a rabbit from a hat.

Wilson starts laughing and I immediately join him. It's a free, unrepentant laugh. Soon we're on the ground with laughter, our asses rolling on the dirty sidewalk and our heads lolling back in the wet grass.

When we finish, we lie there and look up. The stars are dimmed by the lights of the city. The constant murmur of traffic muffles the sound of a conversation outside a fast-food joint down the street, but still we can hear that people are joking, laughing with one another. It all seems perfect and right.

"Thank you, God. Thank you," I say.

"You're welcome," Wilson says.

I laugh at him and push him. He gives a playful punch back, and we laugh again. This laugh ebbs quicker, and we walk to the car. The impact of the alcohol is gone, but I feel more buzzed than ever before.

Chapter 4

Wilson has to be at work an hour before I do, so he's out the door first. He tells me to lock up when I leave. His parents are gone for the same vague reasons as always. St. Louis this time.

Last night I hatched a plan to make it with Lauryn. Or at least spend the night with her. I told my folks I was staying at Frank Schottlemeyre's—he works at the Dairy Castle with me, and I said if I stayed over he could give me a ride in the morning. They should know I'd never stay at Frank's. He's oily and pimply and still can't get his voice to stop breaking even though he'll be a junior. But they'll believe anything if it means they don't have to play chauffeur.

For her part, Lauryn had arranged a place for us. Her friend Amy was on vacation with her parents and had left her a key. It was on. Lauryn insisted that there would be no sex, nothing of the sort. Just spending the night together—*It will be almost like we're married*, she said. *Yeah*, I said, *almost*. Despite her warning, I thought to lift a six-pack from my dad and try to see how far I could get.

I didn't get far. A disaster is what it was. The third time I tried to get my hand up her shirt, she kicked me out. I suddenly had no place to stay, a deep worry that I might lose my girl-friend, and several beers in hand. I decided to stop by Wilson's. He had more beer and plenty of cigarettes as a salve for my pride.

I'm wanting sleep now, but Wilson never seems to need it. He's bright and alert for Wednesday morning on the paint crew. The paint crew is steady nine-to-five Monday-through-Friday. Not like the Dairy Castle, which is whenever the hell they seem to want me. It did not occur to me what kind of imposition a job would force upon my summer.

The job itself provides decent money, but I hate that anyone can see me, the whole town stopping in for cones and sundaes and milk shakes, nachos and tacos and coneys. And there's me, scrambling around like a fool to serve them, sweating and fumbling with the ingredients. Every time I mess up, it feels like headline news. Mr. Lydle, the boss, isn't afraid to call kids out, either. If I don't serve something right, he'll come storming out of the kitchen — he can see everything from back there — huffing and snorting like a Clydesdale, and yell that I've got it all wrong. That it goes ice cream, then chocolate, then nuts, then caramel. Not the caramel first.

As if that could possibly matter.

He did it once in front of Amber and her friends, and it was all I could do to keep my fist from him.

I doubt I will last the summer.

Before I go to work I stop by Lauryn's. She's up already, study-ing. Her dad lets her work summers in his office, but her mother insists that she take summer studies as well. Last summer it was a simple reading list. This summer, Spanish.

It amazes me that she studies even during the summer. With a conscience like that she'll never be idle for long.

She lets me in but won't look at me. Sitting at the kitchen table, doused in morning light, she keeps her nose buried in her book.

"What do you want, Gary?"

"Why do you have to say it like that? I'm your boyfriend. Can't I stop by before I go to work without getting that tone from you?"

She lifts her head from her book. There is no hostility in her face. She's so much better than me at staying calm about things. Even when I know I'm wrong with her, I wind up being the one who gets short, angry, and stupid.

"I didn't try to have any *tone*. I'm sorry."

She turns back to her book, and it just breaks my heart—splits me open inside when she won't even look at me. During school, we'd study together, but we could never keep to our books. We'd get lost in each other, in conversation, our little dreams of getting out of this town, creating a fantasy life. It took us hours to get through one subject, but we were happy to get distracted—even Lauryn didn't mind not keeping to the books. Everything we talked about seemed exciting and new, flooded with potential for both of us. Anything seemed possible.

Now, it's like the summer is pulling us taut, like we might snap, and Lauryn is reacting by keeping her head down in a book, refusing to indulge any distraction.

"Last night," she says, "could have been so nice. Why did you have to ruin it?"

"I'm sorry," I say.

36

"You can't make everything happen all at once, Gary. We're only fifteen. Why can't you just be okay with me? Stop being in such a rush with everything."

"I'm sorry."

"I know. You said."

I sit next to her then and help her practice some words, try to re-create the mood we used to have. I don't try to distract her, though. When she's stumped she closes her eyes, her brows falling into thin slants. She always gets the word right, though, plucking it from its little cove in her mind.

Lauryn's grades shame mine. It's no surprise; she is always one of the best in any class. But she encourages me, telling me that I'm smart enough to beat even her. *When you put your mind to something*, she says, *you always do better than me.*

She stops reciting her words.

"Don't you have to get to work?"

"Sure. Whenever. I can hang out."

"Gary, don't blow the first job you ever had."

I feel like she's pushing me out, just when we were so close to sinking back into that comfort we used to enjoy. I don't mind being late to work if it means enjoying time with her, even for just a few more minutes.

"But I'd rather stay here."

"*Don't* use me as an excuse. Go, Gary."

She puts her hand on mine and I can tell she's not really mad—she's just making a point. I blush, softened by her touch. In a few seconds I'm at the door, and she gives me a kiss on the lips, snapping electricity all through my veins.

For now, that seems just enough, and as I pedal toward work I curse myself for not seeing things that way last night.

Frank and I are both late, and Mr. Lydle is waiting at the back door for us.

"Ten A.M." he says. "Not quarter after. Not five after. Hell, not one after. The way you two mope around, we need every second we can get to prepare."

It only took me a week to learn to return his stare and take it like a man. This concept is lost on Frank, though. He starts stammering excuses.

"Mr. Lydle, I was going to be on time, but I forgot my apron back at the house, and . . ."

"Dammit, son. We've got more aprons. We give you one so you can put it in the laundry and use it all summer, but we can find an extra. Dammit. We need you here on time."

"But." Frank's voice cracks on the word, and it crumbles into three squeaking syllables. He doesn't attempt any more words, just lets his plea hang there.

Lydle just lets go a gravelly sigh.

It takes all of five minutes for Frank to get in trouble again. His excuse about his apron doesn't wash because, of course, he still forgot to bring it. Lydle throws Frank a new one and lets it pass with a few harumphs and *dammits* under his breath, but Lydle's wife, Marny, is the angry one this time.

Marny's old—I don't know how old, but she totters about delicately and seems a decade worse for wear than her husband—and does more harm than good in the kitchen. She adds cheese to burritos when it's supposed to be held, leaves potatoes in the microwave so long they burst, and drops orders from her shaky fingers.

Still, it's good not to cross her. Lydle angers easy but forgets it by the time he gets to the next task. Marny holds grudges. I'm lucky. She likes me. She calls me Jerry instead of Gary half the time, but she likes me.

Lydle sends me outside to wash down the benches and, of course, I don't do it right. I go board by board, scrubbing meticulously. I watch how the wood changes hues as the water seeps in deeper. There's a slight chill to the morning, the summer relenting for a day, and I shiver each time I dip my cloth into the bucket.

Soon, Lydle is beside me. He comes waddling out, his body fat and jiggling with too many years of eating his own products for lunch.

"It's not a Picasso. Just wash the benches down. You have to hustle a little bit, dammit."

He jerks the rag from me and sloshes the water onto the bench. The suds roll off in streams as he washes the table in a quick flurry. It takes him all of five seconds and then he lumbers to the next bench, the bucket clanging against his knee like a tolling bell. I follow him and watch him repeat the mad wash, sweat rolling down under the scraggled gray hair at his temples.

"There," he says. "It's not so damn difficult, is it? Now finish the rest of these up and get inside to help Frank before we open."

He grumbles angrily, and it reminds me for a moment of my dad. But Lydle's complaints have order to them, a beginning and end, unlike the unbridled expanse of my dad's constant anger. If you do what Lydle says, he'll stop yelling.

* * *

We've conquered the lunch rush. The only customers now are coming in for afternoon ice cream. A cone here, a milk shake there. This is the easiest time of all, and I lazily clean the counter. I make a procedure of it, taking my hand in long sweeps of the counter and combing the bits of cheese, meat, and tortilla into my cupped hand. Then I walk to the garbage can and clap my hands over it, getting every last bit into it.

Lydle's up front, cleaning the ice-cream bin and the dull blades of the milk-shake machine. He watches me over the counter and I expect another lecture on the pace of my work.

Instead, he says, "See, now this time of day ain't too bad, is it?"

"I guess not, no."

Marny emerges from the kitchen with vanilla Cokes for both of us. Even Frank, who's taking his lunch break back in the kitchen, seems more at ease.

"How long have you two run this store?" I ask.

"Oh, longer than you been alive," Lydle rasps. Even when he's just chatting he sounds perturbed.

"We opened in 1958," Marny answers. "Now, Gary, it's not easy to stay in business this long. Our daughter tried managing a place over in Indianapolis, but it just didn't go. You have to build a reputation with your customers."

I nod in understanding.

"Oh, hell," Lydle says. "It's just that people won't stay with anything these days. Soon as it gets hard they just give up. And I don't mean just you kids. I might have to growl at you now and then, but you kids aren't too bad. It's the whole damn society."

40

"I know," Marny chimes. "You can't depend on anything these days. Just look at what's happening at Dana."

"Well, that's different, Marny. That's just business. You gotta take care of the bottom line."

My ears perk at this. "What's going to happen there?" I ask.

"They're gone," Lydle intones. "Ain't said it yet, but they're gone. Companies like that don't just threaten to move—they actually do it. I'll bet our entire summer profits on it."

I look out the window and see a haze linger on the parking lot. The Dairy Castle sits on a Y in the road. In the acute angle of the intersection is a liquor store that advertises itself as "The Crotch" because of its location. On the other side of the street is a McDonald's and next to us is an auto maintenance shop. In summer, this is the busiest intersection in town, and each day there are several close calls. We hear cars screech to a stop, horns blaring warnings.

Now, in mid-afternoon, the intersection is subdued. A few cars are in the liquor store lot and two others sit patiently in the fast-food drive-thru. Down the street, though, I see a familiar car approaching. It seems to float along like a long black dash on the street before I bring it into focus for what it is: Roverson's Lincoln.

I know Wilson doesn't get off work until five, so it's not him out for an early joyride. When the blinker flashes next to our drive, unease rises from my toes and floods my body. My limbs and waist feel damp and sticky.

I walk to the kitchen and ask Frank to cover for me, to let me take lunch now. He declines.

"C'mon, Frank. I'm hungry."

He shakes his head at me, still chewing on his burrito. "I'm still eating. I've got fifteen minutes left on break," he says. His voice is a high whine, and melted cheese droops from his mouth.

"Loser," I say. Frank's no good. Even if he were out front he'd screw something up, and I'd have to come help. I wish I could call Wilson, get some advice for escape from this jam.

"Customer," Marny calls. "We need you up here, Jerry."

"Gary," I say. I do it nicely.

"Ooooh. I know. Gary Keeling. I'm sorry, Gary."

She smiles at me as I walk toward her, then shoots a scowl at Frank.

I look out front and my throat constricts. In comes Roverson, the first I've seen him since the story with Lindy popped. For the last month of school he took a leave, and I didn't realize how often I saw him until he was gone. I never had him for class, but his figure was striking. He stood a full six-foot-five and had the ripped features of an athlete even though he was pushing forty. His skin always had color, even in winter.

But now, as he walks to the door, I do a double take to make sure it's him. His flesh bulges beneath his eyes and jaw, and his skin lacks color. A mild slope bends his broad shoulders.

He smiles feebly at Mr. Lydle when he walks to the counter. He leans forward and orders. I can see him, but he hasn't looked back to my station.

"Two hot!" I hear Lydle call to me.

I start the tacos and try to hide my face behind the microwave. I'm terrified to let Roverson see me. My face will let him know everything.

When the microwave sounds, I pull out the tacos and fold them. Lydle comes back and stands next to me.

"You give him the food," he says. "I'm not handing a damn thing to that guy."

"I can't believe he has the nerve to show his face in town," Marny says.

I start to protest, stammering excuses not to face Roverson. I even feign the same disgust the Lydles show. It's to no avail, though. Lydle demands I serve Roverson, and he walks back to the kitchen with his wife, still haranguing about the customer waiting out front.

I slouch out with the tacos. Staring down at the Formica, I watch my feet shuffle one in front of the other. When I set the tacos on the counter wordlessly, I see Roverson's big hand reach out to take them, scooping both up in his meaty fingers.

Frank and Marny and Lydle are talking in the kitchen, and I can hear their voices bleed out in indistinguishable syllables. Under that sound, I hear Roverson's steps toward the door. My head is still down, and I wait to hear the door open before I lift it. I wait, but there is no squeak of the door. I wait, wait, wait. No door. He's standing there just watching me. I wait some more. Still no door. I can feel his presence. I can feel eyes on me.

My head lifts as if against my own will. And when my eyes finally absorb the room in front of me, I see Roverson still standing at the door, staring back.

He smiles.

He pushes against the door with his back.

Before he turns to leave he does something so quick I can't even be sure it happens. But I think what I see is Roverson winking at me.

*   *   *

The incinerator always marks the end of my shift. It's not really an incinerator—it's three brick walls with a pile of ash sitting in the center, more like an open-air fireplace. There's no roof on it, either, so the smoke just spirals right out. But Lydle calls it the incinerator and always sends me out to burn the disposables before I go home for the day.

I suspect there are things in here I'm not supposed to burn. Every day it's a heap of egg cartons and plastic tortilla wrappers among the wasted food and soiled paper towels. It's Lydle's orders, though. I figure it's his ass if anything ever happens.

Today it's a particularly heavy load. Frank continually messes up orders, and they all wind up in the incinerator. *Hey, Frank,* Lydle will say. *Next time I'm gonna have Gary take your paycheck out there with all that wasted food.* Frank never has anything to say to this, just his jaw hanging open and his eyes threatening tears. He is so easy to dislike.

I walk out the back door with the trash and look around, almost expecting Roverson to be there waiting for me. I can't wait to tell Wilson. As bizarre as Roverson's acknowledgment was, it reignited the rush I felt the first time we lifted his ride.

I dump the piles on top of the dead ash and reach for the book of matches. They're thick and industrial, like miniature trees between my fingers.

"Hey, Gary."

It's Lydle, hustling out to catch me before I strike the match.

"Gary, do you have any friends still looking for summer jobs?"

"Not really. I think all the kids I know are pretty settled in for the summer. Why?"

He looks both ways, like he's about to cross the street.

"Marny's pretty fed up with Frank. I always say give the kid another chance, but when she makes up her mind, well. It's not a done deal yet, but I'm trying to anticipate another open slot."

He stares down apologetically. Every summer, kids shuffle through here like tourists, chased off by his growling and sour moods. Yet he feels bad when his wife wants him to ax Frank.

"I'll ask around," I say.

That satisfies him, and he says he'll see me on my next shift. He shuffles back inside, his back hunched under years of employees like Frank.

I turn back to the incinerator and light the trash. One motion is all it takes—I've perfected a single sweep that strikes the match to the box and sends it tumbling, lit, toward the trash, but slow enough that it stays lit for impact. I light a few more just to get the blaze up faster. Lydle instructs me to always stay until it dies down, in case it gets out of control. Of course, he's never given me a plan for what to do in case the flames do spill over the walls. Around the incinerator, a few inches of cement serve as a barrier to the grass, which is tamped and dead, leaving mostly dirt. Above it, though, tree limbs hang dangerously close.

The fire rises, and the blanket of its heat wraps around me. Sparks snap like the tail of a whip, popping upward near the leaves. Small wisps of black smoke curl in the center, the poisons of some foul waste rising into the summer air.

The day is muggy and windless, not a ripe afternoon for a fire to spread.

Still, with the heat rolling over me in waves—hotter than any summer Indiana can offer—I feel certain that everything is about to combust.

Chapter 5

Wilson waits for my mother to go back upstairs, then dumps a stream of rum into the Cokes she brought us.

"Your mom's all right, you know that?"

"Whatever."

"No, I mean she's *all right*."

I know he's messing; he used to get under my skin this way, implying that he had the hots for my mom. It's an old joke now, and it can't work on me anymore.

"Just call a play," I say.

"Touchy, touchy." He takes a sip from his Coke and lets go a big *aahhhhhh*. He smacks his lips.

"I'm not being touchy. You're just trying to change the subject so I don't beat your ass again."

We're playing video football, the only thing I consistently beat Wilson in. Real sports, connecting with girls, general excitement: He's got me covered in all those areas. But I get him on video games nine times out of ten. It doesn't diminish his confidence, though.

"I'm coming right at you this time. I'm running right over your ass."

"Bring it, Wilson. Bring it."

This time, though, he does just as he says—barrels through me and into the end zone. Immediately, Wilson drops the controller and raises his hands over his head in a victorious pose. Then he points at me.

"You, you, you," he says, almost barking it.

I laugh at him. I'm still up three scores but it doesn't matter to Wilson. If I point out the score he'll simply say, *You're only as good as your last play, son*, so I let him have his fun.

The mood is easy between us, and I like the fact that we're just doing this: staying in, playing video games, avoiding—except for the liquor Wilson smuggled in—any real trouble. It used to be like this more often. Our pleasures and our crimes were simpler: It wasn't always drinking and stealing cars. It used to be video games, one-on-one basketball, riding our bikes. At worst all we needed for a grand time was a carton of eggs to throw at the fraternities and our own two feet to make the getaway.

It never seemed dangerous, and even the guys chasing us would be laughing half the time, like it was all part of the game—townie kids throw a few eggs, the frat boys come chasing after them in the night, acting tough, trying to corner them in an alley or the nearby woods. The one time we did get caught, we just agreed to clean up the mess, and then they let us hang out and play video games with them for a few hours. Of course, two weeks later we were back at it again, this time toilet-papering their lawn in the middle of the night. And again they chased us, screaming all kinds of empty threats and trying to hide their laughter—all like a well-rehearsed play where nobody could really get hurt.

Once Wilson settles back in, he kicks the ball back to me,

and I start on a drive. Wilson hates defense, and I always know if I can get a few first downs he'll get bored and start chasing me blindly, making it even easier for me to score. I know I can frustrate him even more by taking my time between plays, using up the clock.

"Today, Gary. Jesus. Call a play already." He sips at his drink impatiently.

I run a play, a run up the middle for just a few yards, and then I wait again. I scroll through all my plays like I'm having trouble deciding. We go through this procedure until I've moved all the way down to his twenty-yard line. I can tell he's barely paying attention to the game anymore, his thoughts wandering along mischievous detours. That's when I decide to really let him have it.

"Guess who I saw the other day, Wilson."

"Who?" He says it dully, like the sound of a shoe being dropped to the floor.

"Roverson."

"You saw who?!" Now his voice rings with excitement, his attention entirely on me, wrestled away from anything else in the room.

Using this opportunity, I snap the ball and go trotting untouched into the end zone. Touchdown. I mimic his pose from earlier, taunting him right back. Wilson drops the controller and leaps at me, driving his shoulder into my gut like a real tackler. We crash onto the floor and Wilson jumps on top of me, his knees pressing against my chest and his index finger giving stiff pokes to my forehead.

"That's cheap, Gary. Cheap, cheap, cheap."

I know he doesn't really give a damn about the game, so I

48

start laughing at him. Even when his pokes start to hurt I know he's just playing. Finally, I squirrel my way from under him and scramble behind the couch, which serves as an island between us.

"I'm gonna knock your ass out," Wilson threatens. We're both laughing, though, our breaths coming in gasps.

"Jump on over here, then, tough guy."

He leaps over the couch, but I'm on the move again, racing back to my controller to try to take further advantage of him when he's not at his. He comes bounding back toward the game, but he doesn't go for his controller. Instead, he switches off the unit, ending the game.

"Awww, Wilson. Why'd you do that? We only had a few minutes left in it."

His face changes from playful to dead-on serious, the corners of his mouth dropping to form an even line. He gives a few last huffs, trying to catch his breath.

"Did you really see Roverson?" he asks.

"Yeah, I did. He came into the Dairy Castle."

We start talking in hushed tones like somebody might be eavesdropping at the base of the stairs, even though my dad isn't home and we can hear my mom walking above us, pots clanging in the kitchen.

"Did he say anything?"

"No. Just placed his order, and I had to bring it out to him. Dumb-ass Frank wouldn't take it out, so I had to face him. And get this. He winked at me."

Wilson's jaw drops open slightly, and his eyes grow wide in a look of surprise that isn't common on his face.

"He winked? How? Like a 'Thanks, kid' wink? Or what?"

I shake my head and sit down on the couch. Wilson squats on the floor to accept the rest of my story.

"No, Wilson. Roverson winked like he *knew*."

We hear my mother's footsteps on the stairwell, and we scramble to turn the game back on, picking up our controllers to assume a pose of normalcy. Not only is the subject of Roverson off-limits because we've been stealing his car, his own actions have tarnished his name. In the spring, the story broke that he and Lindy had been having an affair. Lindy was eighteen—as Wilson says, *a legal little Hoosier*—but the news didn't go over well at school, with the town in general, and specifically, with Lindy's parents. By the end of the semester, Roverson was fired, and Lindy was sent packing to her aunt's place up in Hammond.

"You two okay down here? I thought I heard some shouts."

I look at her in a way I hope tells her to *scram, my friend's here*, but she doesn't seem to notice, just stands there with a dishrag in her hand, a drop of water gathering on its corner. I've seen old pictures of her from her yearbooks, and there was an undeniable life about her. She was a cheerleader, her hair pulled back in a ponytail to let her smile and her eyes stand out. Now, though, I don't see any of that life. She's thin, her face beginning to crease in wrinkles, and it's as if something vital, some piece of her soul, disappeared.

"We're just playing video games," I finally say.

"Gary keeps cheating, Mrs. Keeling," Wilson says. "I had to knock him around a little bit." He has a way of joking with adults that doesn't seem patronizing to them. It's not that he tries to put on a good, flattering front. The opposite, really. He's never pretended to be a good kid, but since he doesn't try to put

50

on an act, most of the teachers seem to respect him, even if they don't like him and the hell he raises.

I worry she can smell the rum on us. I take a whiff myself, trying to determine if I can catch a trace lingering in the room. I can, but I know it's there, and I wonder if it's just my imagination. Surely, she senses something. Despite our innocent looks, I keep expecting her instinct to kick in. Or maybe she doesn't want to smell it, to sense it, to assume deeper troubles than the ones she already has.

"Okay, then. Just try to keep it down. Gary, I'm going to try to take a nap before your father gets home."

She turns and walks back to the stairs, a few drops of water spotting the carpet where she stood. She moves silently, her feet used to walking gingerly. As soon as she disappears, Wilson is back on me, pressing the subject adamantly.

"Okay, okay. So Roverson winked at you. Are you sure? How do you know he *knew*?"

"First, he definitely winked. And second, I know something's up, because he waited for me to look at him. He lingered by the door, and I could kind of feel his eyes on me. Then when I looked up—*bam*—he winked right at me."

Wilson claps his hands together and begins to rub them back and forth, like he is trying to warm them. I wonder if he's as worried about it as I am, the potential for being found out. The trouble we'll be in. I think again about Lauryn and know she'll flip if she finds out what we've been doing.

Then Wilson starts to grin. "You know that's about the first anyone's seen him since the whole thing with Lindy went down. Man is shunned. Like he doesn't exist. This is getting interesting now, Gary."

I can see a small excitement in Wilson begin to smolder, flare into a larger flame. *I don't want this*, I think. Just one afternoon with things going smoothly, that's all I want. Video games and putting on good faces for my mom. That's all.

"I don't see the big deal about Lindy," Wilson says. "Not like he was the only one knocking it with her. Girl was friendly, Gary. Friendly to me, at least."

"You lie," I say. I want to divert him, take his mind away from Roverson onto something else. "When did you get busy with Lindy?"

"When didn't I?" he answers. There is no stopping his swagger when it comes to conquests of girls. Even if half of his claims are made up, I've never seen him let on that any of them are anything but the sacred truth. "Forget Lindy. We gotta get back to Roverson's."

"What?"

"Back. We gotta hit Roverson's again and find out what he's all about."

I knew when I saw his excitement rise he was headed in that direction, but still it hits me with surprising force, the way an alarm clock can jar you even when you know it's set to go off. I try to keep my voice stable and calming.

"Wilson, do you really think that's a good idea? Sounds like a surefire way to get arrested. You don't really want that, do you?"

"No, Gary. I don't want to get arrested. But don't you know me well enough to know that won't happen? I just want to rile the guy."

"No way," I say.

He puts his hands on his hips. "It's too tempting not to. Damn, man. Where's your will? If it was up to you we'd just sit around and play video games every day. Now, don't get me wrong. This is all good and fine. But we need to shake things up a bit."

There's no stopping him. He sets his mind to a course and it's like he has blinders, with only the finish line in his vision. Inside me I can feel a surrender starting, the tip of my will crumbling away, and I know soon all my resistance will dissolve, spread out and useless like a spilled packet of salt.

"Okay," I say. "Fine. But just tell me one thing."

"Whatever you want, Gary,"

"Did you really get it on with Lindy?"

Wilson just starts laughing, bellowing in a voice as robust as someone twice, three times his age. I start to laugh, too. The truth is, I'd love to pin Wilson down on the truth about Lindy, but I'm suddenly caught up in his laugh too much to care. I feel light with the humor of it, the insanity of all of it.

"What's so funny down there?" It's my mother again, and even though we're making too much noise again, her voice seems to carry a lilt, like our laughter is contagious, its perky drug floating up through the house floor by floor.

"Gary's telling dirty jokes," Wilson calls up. "I don't know where he gets such filthy stuff." He does this while unscrewing the cap again on the bottle, tilting it toward me in an offer.

"I don't believe you for a second, Wilson. My baby's way too sweet for that. I think maybe you're the one. You're the one, I say." Even behind her accusation, though, we can hear suppressed laughter.

Outside, I can hear a car pull up: my dad. Mom shuts the door to downstairs then. I hear her feet tracking back to the kitchen above us.

I look at Wilson and make one last vain plea. "Seriously, Wilson. I don't think we should go back there. The guy's gonna call the cops before long."

"You might be right," he says. He rubs his chin like he's really considering my warning. "Shoot, Gary. If you think he might call the cops soon, we should probably do something before he does—we better go tonight!" He smiles then, unstoppable and beaming.

We seal it on a swig of rum and shake hands, making it somehow official. Upstairs I hear the door open, and I can make out the bass of my father's voice.

Chapter 6

Dad walks slowly, his feet sounding like softballs dropped one by one on the floor—*thud, thud, thud.* When he gets above us, where my mother is, we hear their voices start to mingle, his coming out in deep rumbles and hers floating above it tentatively.

Wilson senses my nervousness, and immediately he starts talking, trying to fill in the silence in the basement while their sounds mix above us in an ugly song.

"C'mon, man. What you wanna do? Play another game? You want to scoot down to Short Stop and get some chips, maybe lift some mags? Hey, I know. Let's grab a porno with a bunch of young girls, that way we can bribe Roverson if things get tight."

I laugh, but my heart's not in it. It's strange how just the sound of my dad's feet, the murmur of his voice, can change everything. Thing is, for all I know he could be in a good mood. It's just that I've learned to assume the worst.

There are times when I try to remember how he used to be. There was a time, when I was a kid, when we got along at least a little bit. I remember throwing a baseball with him until the sky went dark, the two of us standing out in the yard seeing the ball in the dim glow of the porch light. I remember him driving us on vacation to New York City when I was six, letting me ride shotgun after my mom was tired and waking me up so I could see the skyline emerge in the night, glowing like some miracle.

But that was all long ago, clouded in deep, tainted waters. I wonder if all that was even real, even the same person. Or maybe it never happened at all. Maybe my mind invents wonder in the past since I can't find any now—a trick to make me give him room for forgiveness.

Wilson keeps after me, though, trying to fish a response—any kind of response—out of me. "Yeah, boy," he says. "We need to pick a few magazines. Only way your ass is gonna see any skin. I *know* you aren't getting any action from Lauryn."

Behind him the television is still flickering, the light flashing and changing behind him as a car salesman screams through the set about a sale nobody can pass up. For a moment, I feel frozen in sound, the commercial dancing underneath the rumblings of my parents, Wilson's comment about Lauryn echoing in my head. Somehow, the timing of it makes me feel betrayed by him, as if he'd singled me out for ridicule in the hallway at school like older kids sometimes do to freshmen and sophomores in spontaneous, whimsical cruelties.

Wilson has a nose for my thoughts, though, and defuses my tension. "Look, Gary," he says. "Never mind that. I was just joking. You get all tight when your pop comes around. I was just trying to get you to relax."

"He's such a bastard," I say.

"Most fathers are."

The door to the stairs swings open again, and with the first heavy footstep I know it's my dad. I sink back into the couch, the springs giving a squeak, and try to pay attention to what's come on television. Old shit—a rerun of some '80s sitcom. I couldn't care less, but I lean forward like I'm absorbed in it. Wilson does likewise as my dad approaches.

"Gary, why haven't you mowed the lawn?" My dad is just steps away from us. His presence feels like a bonfire in the room, sparks popping off and landing on my skin.

I don't answer, just lean closer to the TV. I pick the remote up from the floor and turn it up a notch.

"Gary."

I shrug. I give a glance over at Wilson, but he's looking straight ahead, calm. He flicks something from his shorts and brushes it down to the floor.

"Gary! Goddammit, answer me. Don't just sit there and shrug. Why the hell didn't you mow the lawn?"

I start to answer but Wilson speaks first. He swings around in his chair, his back now to the TV. His leg swings over the arm and his face has the same defiant steel to it that he gives me when he's trying to coerce me into something.

"We were just watching television. Playing video games. Gary kept saying he had to go mow the lawn, but I kept talking him out of it. I guess, if anything, it's my fault."

I turn to catch my dad's reaction to Wilson—at first his eyes are still on me, but they make a long, slow, tiresome blink and then shift over to Wilson, a heat rising in them.

"You think you're big, don't you, kid? A mouth like that might bite off more than it can chew." He pauses and turns up a corner of his mouth, shifts his eyes back and forth between us.

I watch Wilson, wondering what he'll do. At school, Wilson is never intimidated by teachers, and the few times I've seen his parents around they float by wordlessly like we're not even there. But now Wilson seems a bit taken aback, like he's not sure how to react to my father. He opens his mouth slightly, but then shuts it again as if he's changed his mind against a comeback.

"Gary, that lawn isn't gonna cut itself," my father continues. "Why you make me tell you a million times, I'll never know. Now snap your ass in gear."

I feel something give inside me, like something breaking, as I bend down obediently for my shoes. That's when I hear Wilson laughing.

Standing just a few feet from my father, Wilson is laughing right at him. His laughs don't come out like he's been struck by anything funny, but more like some rhythmic, purposeful defiance of my father. My dad eyes Wilson again and takes a threatening step toward him.

"Something funny, son?" he asks Wilson.

"Shit, man," Wilson says, drawing multiple syllables out of *shit*. "I guess you just don't know."

My father explodes. "What the hell does that mean, you little prick? You think you can talk like that to me in my house? You say one more word and I will teach you a lesson your sorry-ass daddy should've taught you long ago!"

Wilson shuts up then and walks to the stairs. As he climbs them, he catches my eye and mouths the word *tonight*.

I start slipping my shoes on in a hurry, wanting to escape the room before my dad can level his anger in my direction. As I do, though, I watch Wilson leave, his sturdy frame walking up the stairs, somehow untainted, unbent by my father's wrath. As I watch him leave I wonder if I'll ever be able to do that, to be that strong. And I wonder, too, what I'll do if he leaves for good, plucked away to Pennsylvania and out of my life forever.

Even after a shower, I can still smell the grass and sweat on me, like it's part of my skin. When I get to Lauryn's I feel almost ill looking at the closed door, knowing what's behind it—good house, good parents, good girl. Goodness, all of it. There's an itch inside me, a suspicion that I'm not worthy of it, that I shouldn't even go inside. Still, my feet go one in front of the other, up the pavement between the perfectly ordered rows of tulips. Even their lawn is better than ours, managed by professionals and treated so it's a lush green instead of the choked, weedy ground that surrounds our house, cut weekly by the rusty old blades on our mower.

I ring the doorbell and wait for someone to answer, watching birds swoop down to perch on the feeder. I feel like an imposter here, like I'll be discovered and expelled at any moment, like Lauryn is always on the verge of giving up on me. Still, she hasn't given up on me yet, and it's a far better option than hanging around my father, waiting for him to find another reason to blow up. By the time I get home, I know he'll be drunk—the question is whether he'll be blanketed in it and too drowsy to do anything but grunt and watch TV, or if it will flick a switch inside him and send him railing against the confines of his house, his town, his life.

Lauryn's mother opens the door, welcomes me with a sincere smile. I can feel the nerves and mistrust inside me start to ease.

"Gary," she says. "How are you today? Come in, come in. Lauryn's upstairs, but sit and visit for a second before you go up."

I mutter out a hello, then follow her into the kitchen and take a seat when she motions to the chair.

"Anything to drink, Gary?"

"No thanks," I say.

She pulls ice from the freezer, drops it into a glass, and slides it in front of me.

"Now, Gary. Just slow down and have a glass of water with me."

She pulls a pitcher from the refrigerator and fills the glasses, sits down next to me. Mrs. Avery moves in brisk, businesslike movements. Like her husband, she addresses me like an adult. With her, though, I appreciate it more than with him. I can imagine her sometimes as an older version of Lauryn.

"How's your summer, Gary?" she asks.

"Fine so far."

"How is Dairy Castle working out? Do you like having a job?"

"Sure, I guess," I say. Something about all this is unsettling. I feel like she has me there for a reason beyond asking about my summer job. She's a lawyer, and I've been around her enough to know that everything she says has a purpose.

"Gary," she says, then pauses. She fingers her earrings, adjusts the collar on her blouse, like she's uncomfortable. She glances at her watch, mutters that she needs to stop by the office today, even on a weekend.

Finally, she looks at me and continues. "I like you, Gary. And Mr. Avery does, too. We know that Lauryn really enjoys you, and you've always been a nice enough boy around us."

I don't know what she's getting at, and my face must betray this to her, because she explains.

"Look, Gary. Just be good to Lauryn. You're both at an impressionable age, and I don't want you . . . pushing her in directions that she's not ready to go in. That neither of you are ready to go in."

I hold up my hands in a plea of ignorance. She takes my water away even though I haven't touched it, walks to rinse it out in the sink, her heels going *click click click* across the linoleum. When she speaks, there is greater authority in her voice and I can tell how serious she is even though she isn't facing me.

"Just go slow with her, Gary. I think you know what I mean."

"Okay," I mutter.

She walks to the edge of the stairs and calls up to tell Lauryn I'm here. Then she turns back to me.

"You can go on up," she says. "I'm leaving for the office at two. But Mr. Avery will be home any minute."

She walks toward the den, pats me on the shoulder as she passes.

When I get into Lauryn's room, she's reading on her bed. Her room is teeming with books, magazines, and stuffed animals. On her bed alone, she is surrounded by a unicorn, a frog, and two bears. From her book, she lifts her eyes to me serenely, her face smoothing into a wide smile.

"Hi, crazy boy," she says.

She hops off her bed and comes over to me, wraps her small arms around my body.

When I don't hug her back, she pulls away.

"What's wrong, Gary?"

I kick at the floor and don't say anything. It's always hard for me to ease into things with Lauryn after any confrontation with my dad. Then, before I know what I'm doing, I reach out and pull her to me, plant a heavy kiss on her lips. Lauryn pushes away, her hands balling into little fists against my ribs, and then backpedals to her bed and sits again, throwing her animals to the floor in disgust.

"What's wrong with you?" she says.

"What? I can't kiss you?"

"Not like that. Not like you're angry."

I look at her walls, decorated with artwork, certificates from school, a cross.

"Well, maybe you should tell me what the hell's up with the third degree from your mom," I finally say. I thrust my hands into my pockets, trying to look like I really don't care even though I'm asking.

"What? What are you talking about, Gary?"

"She was just down there giving me a lecture about you. About how I'm taking you in the wrong direction. What did you tell her?"

Lauryn stares up at me, her eyes quivering. As I spoke, I walked closer to her so that now I'm less than a foot from where she's sitting.

She dips her head away from me, gives me a hesitant, "Well . . ."

"Well, what? What, Lauryn, what?" I feel my voice rising, and I check myself before it goes into an all-out yell. The last thing I need is Mr. or Mrs. Avery popping up here now.

Lauryn answers in nearly a whisper: "I told my mom about what happened the other night. How you wanted me to sleep with you."

"Shit, Lauryn! How could you do that to me? What the hell were you thinking?" I can just see her parents' reaction, their front of respecting me undermined entirely, confirmed in the doubts about me that I've always suspected they harbor.

This time, though, Lauryn doesn't respond in a whisper. Instead, she stands and fires back at me, inches from my face.

"Don't you dare blame this on me, Gary. Look, I like you, but it's like it's just one thing with you, like if I won't have sex with you then I'm not even worth your time. And I'm sick of it. I'm sick of being treated that way, and I'm sick of feeling guilty when it's not my fault."

Her anger catches me off guard, and even though she's right I know I won't admit it. I have too much frustration already without surrendering to her, without letting go of the last remnants of my pride.

"Fine," I say. "Be that way. Hell, maybe Wilson's right. Maybe I should be hitting on Amber instead. It sure would be easier than banging my head against a wall with you."

Lauryn's face turns down, the fire that was there extinguishing. She goes silent and looks away from me. A hurt seems to flow out of her, and I know immediately how stupid it was for me to say that.

"Just go," she says.

I turn to leave without another word. The long road of yet another apology, of making things right with Lauryn, begins to stretch out in front of me—and it looks longer than ever before. I'd cut off my own hands to have a chance to undo the last ten

63

minutes, but I can't be that lucky. The thing is, no matter how much I just messed up, Lauryn will afford me another chance. It's just that I know I keep racking up emotional debt with her, so that someday I'll go in so deep there's no way she'll ever forgive me.

I say nothing to Mrs. Avery, who is still in the kitchen, but when I head out the door I see Mr. Avery coming up the drive. I look straight at him, beaming my best fake smile. It's the only way I can hold back the scream swelling inside.

Chapter 7

I don't tell Wilson about what happened with Lauryn, but he must be able to tell that I'm bothered by something: He's been almost too nice to me tonight. Maybe he just thinks that I'm still on edge from the run-in with my dad this morning.

"You okay, Gary?" he asks.

I nod, but it's not convincing. Wilson gives me a playful backhand into my stomach. I flinch, but when he makes contact I can feel that his hand simply bounces off the muscles in my stomach. Physically, it seems I'm growing stronger every day, but I know less and less how to harness it.

"Damn, jumpy," Wilson says. "You can't be that nervous. Lighten up, Gary."

I give him a dull look, and he can tell I'm not easily cheered tonight.

"Look, son, I can't have you sulking. Now cheer up before I knock some sense into you."

"Not funny," I say.

We're standing among the soybeans again, the stalks noticeably higher than the first time we crept out to Roverson's. The summer is in full bloom now, near the end of June.

"Sorry, Gary. But sometimes I feel like I need to give you a jump start to have any fun. Hell, you sure wouldn't be here tonight if it weren't for me. Now let's go."

We start our creep across the street to Roverson's. The thrill, which was waning as our car theft became routine, is back in full force now that Roverson might be onto our scheme. We didn't even bother to drink tonight, using the buzz from our nervousness to fuel us instead.

Once again we crouch and make our approach and, once again, we take our positions by the Lincoln, listening to the insects making a symphony out of their sounds, our eyes alert for any movements along the road or from the house. It's strange how relaxed we had become. The last time we took the Lincoln, we barely even paused to look for lights along the road, barely took caution in our sounds. It seemed, in fact, like it wasn't theft it all. We almost felt like it was *our* car, and the bike ride, the hike across the field, the secrecy were all simply inconveniences.

Now, however, my pulse is racing again. And despite Wilson's constant cool, I can see an urgency evident in his motions. All it took was for Roverson to make the slightest push into the comfort of our lives for us to realize what an intrusion we'd made into his. More than ever, I feel like there are certain consequences to what I'm doing tonight, even if they remain cloaked in a deep, unhinting disguise.

"You ready, Gary?"

"No. But I'm pretty sure that doesn't make a difference."

"That's my boy."

Wilson puts his hand on the door handle and takes a deep breath as he readies to enter. Crouched by the tire, my post to look for oncoming traffic, I quickly ask Wilson if he's nervous at all.

"Of course I am," he answers. He flashes a smile of bravado to me. "That's the whole point of this, right? If it doesn't cook our nerves, it isn't worth doing."

Wilson makes his dive into the car and reaches up to kill the overhead light in one smooth, practiced motion. On the outside, a breeze kicks up and I feel a small chill from it—nice relief from the sweltering night, but it makes me want to be anywhere but here right now. I stare into the darkness toward town and see it producing a small layer of light above it in the sky, like a halo—only there's never been anything holy about Dearborn Springs.

Down the road the other way there is no light, only a hot, dark distance. Somewhere out there, toward Terre Haute and then Illinois and then St. Louis and then the expanse of the west—anywhere, really, beyond Dearborn Springs—I imagine people living real lives, kids my age who don't have to resort to juvenile delinquency for entertainment. I imagine purpose, something I can't seem to find here.

I can't keep my mind on those things, though. It's been a full minute since Wilson entered the car, and by now he's usually located the keys and is ready to start rolling the Lincoln away. Torn between keeping my watch and abandoning it to see what's the matter inside the car, I feel myself start to sweat even more. The breeze is gone and the night is settling over me, pressing down like a body, like my father's weight pressing on me. *What's taking him so long?* I think. *Can't he find the keys? Is he just trying to scare me? Did he hurt himself somehow when he dove into the car?* It's too much. I poke my head around the open door.

"Wilson! What the hell's going on?"

In the darkness he's reclined in the driver's seat like someone cruising leisurely through town, a small grin on his face and a scrap of paper in his right hand.

"No keys in here," he says. "But I know where they are."

"What the hell are you talking about?"

"Here," he says, and hands me the piece of paper.

He flips on the overhead light so I can read it, but I immediately shut it off.

"Wilson! You want to get us busted? Keep that damn light off."

He just laughs and tells me to quit sweating everything, tells me I'll see what's going on soon enough. After the flash of the light, it takes my eyes a bit to readjust to the darkness. There are small tracers lingering in the corners of my vision, and I have to pull the note out into the moonlight to read it. The whole time my nerves are just growing with intensity. When I bend my head down to the note a bead of sweat rolls off my nose and hits the paper with a tiny *thwack*.

I feel Wilson's breath over my shoulder as he leans in to read the note again with me. With a good deal of squinting, my eyes finally focus on the letters on the paper, printed in perfect, rigid penmanship.

THERE'S NO NEED TO SNEAK AROUND WHEN YOU'VE ALREADY BEEN DISCOVERED, the note begins. IF YOU WANT THE CAR, COME IN AND ASK FOR THE KEYS. BE POLITE ABOUT IT.

Unlike the printed message, the cursive signature is hard to decipher, but I know already what it says: William Roverson.

My feet hit the gravel and start me racing toward the field, carried swiftly by pure fear. In my mind, I see Roverson, police, teachers, supervisors, parents, girlfriend, and girlfriend's parents all gathered for one big confrontation on the other side of Roverson's dark door. I split so fast it takes even Wilson a while to catch me, tackle me, and pin me to the ground. When I stand up, I see I've covered more than half the soybean field in my flight. We're only twenty yards from our bikes.

Tempted to run again, I stop myself, knowing that Wilson will only catch me and tackle me again. I brush the dirt from my elbows and knees and try to catch my breath.

"I suppose you're dead set on going in there and getting those keys," I say.

"Not dead set on it, but I'm not ready to turn tail like a pussy just yet."

His words come at me like a dare, and his tone seeks its way under my skin. When I pause, he sees an opening and follows up the dare with a softer sell.

"Look, Gary. Let's at least discuss this. You know, son, the pros and cons."

"Fuck that," I say. "You can't talk me into it this time, Wilson. I'm cutting my losses and going home."

"Wait, wait. Gary. What's the worst that could happen?"

"Being arrested! How about that, Wilson? What about being grounded for the rest of my teenage life? Those are the cons. I don't see any pros."

I turn to walk, but he grabs my arm and spins me around again. My arm is so sweaty that his hand just slides right down it until it sticks at the knot of my wrist.

"Damn, Gary. What about the car?"

"What about it?"

"The guy could be telling the truth. What if we can get his car with no hassle?"

We stand there in the moonlit field, both of us huffing from our run, and hash it out. I keep pleading with Wilson to leave Roverson alone, to call it a night, but my argument loses steam with every word. Wilson listens to me patiently, attentively, and when I finish speaking he gives a long pause, seeming to consider the factors in the decision confronting us.

"I hear you, Gary. I do. And I'm not gonna lie and say this whole night doesn't make me anxious. But, dammit, fact is that fucker threw down a challenge to us."

"That doesn't mean we have to take him up on it, Wilson," I say.

"Like hell, Gary." He grabs my wrist again and we begin marching back toward the house. "We absolutely have to. That's the only way we can live. Someone like that draws a line in the sand, and it's our duty to cross it."

At the door, we both pause. Even Wilson is showing signs of fear, flicking his hair back from his eyes and biting his lip.

The circumstances that pushed Roverson from school are not nearly as offensive to us as they were to the rest of the town. Still, I can't help but consider what people would think if they saw us readying to enter his house. Here's a man who got busted for sleeping with one of his students, and even if I'd give three fingers to get that same chance with a girl like Lindy, I'm swayed by the town's disgust, like I'm obligated to share its shame.

When the story of Roverson and Lindy got out, we found it shocking. Roverson always had his act together, his classes run with a rigid precision, his clothes creased just so, his muscles obviously the product of a strict workout schedule. Most of the guys in school envied him; the girls, in turn, flirted with him. While our other teachers were objects of ridicule, like they belonged in an older, foolish world, Roverson was worthy of admiration, even among the most cynical students. It was hard to believe someone as ordered and structured as Roverson would let things fall apart around him like that.

Still, it somehow makes sense at the same time. Wilson always suspected that there was something *too* perfect about Roverson, that he had to have a crack in him just like everyone else. And, looking back, the temptation he must have felt from all the constant flirting of girls like Lindy must have been hard to resist.

Everything I thought about him, though, is revised with the knowledge of his affair. And while I remember his immaculate appearance, it now seems almost sinister, like it was all part of an illusion he'd been performing. On top of that, his pasty and hollow looks—the way he appeared to be a shell of his old self—the other day in the Dairy Castle worry me. What is Roverson really about? What do we really know about the people who teach us every day? What do we know about anybody?

With me and Wilson poised at his door, all these thoughts race through my mind. The door, a big brown slab of silence, reveals nothing. There is only the faintest glimmer of light coming from behind the drawn curtains beside it. What other secrets lurk behind that door? What else is Roverson hiding?

Before I can start to form possible answers to these questions, Wilson has pressed the doorbell, the cold, metallic sound disrupting the hot night. My throat starts to constrict and I feel almost nauseous, the impulse to run hitting me again. Wilson, though, positions himself right next to me, ready to grab me at the slightest hint of retreat. In the stillness after the doorbell's chime, I listen for hints of life inside but can barely make anything out above the crickets and cicadas—perhaps there's the murmur of a TV or radio, a few bumps that could be footsteps, maybe some rustling of papers, and then, I think, a cough.

I'm leaning in, ear almost to the door when it suddenly opens, Roverson unlatching it and swinging it open quickly. His massive frame fills the entrance. There is darkness behind him, and the moonlight slips onto the porch to shine on his chalky fingers, the milky flesh above his collar, his high, sad cheekbones.

"I thought you two were going to wait out here forever," he says. His rumbling voice still sounds as confident as ever, even if he appears sickly. "I thought I heard you out by the car almost twenty minutes ago."

For the first time I can remember, Wilson is speechless. His jaw hangs open, and I recognize the look of intimidation on his face: It's what I imagine I look like when I can't find out how to respond to my father.

"So?" Roverson says.

It's enough to get Wilson going again.

"What's up, Roverson?" he asks, dropping the *Mr.* as if he weren't talking to him at all but referring to him in another conversation.

"That's *Mr.* Roverson. You're Wilson England, right? And Gary Keeling? Let's get this first thing straight—since I've given you the generous measure of not turning you over to the local law enforcement, you *will* treat me with respect. Is that understood?"

"Yes," we both mutter.

"Not much enthusiasm there. But good enough. So, are you two going to come in?"

He doesn't wait for our answer. Instead he turns and goes back inside, sinking into the darkness of his house. I look at Wilson, begging with my eyes not to follow, but he just flashes me a devilish grin and crosses the threshold, lifting his right foot high and stomping into the house with a loud *thump*.

When we get into the living room, we see that the television is on with no sound. Papers and envelopes are scattered on the floor helter-skelter. This place is a mess even compared to my room. It has the look of something that hasn't been disturbed in decades, like we are stumbling into some archaeological find. It has a musty, sour smell, like fruit gone bad.

Roverson brushes loose stacks of paper from a couple chairs and tells us to sit down. At a desk, adorned with various cans of beer and soda, he finds a lamp switch to give the room more light. The clearer the picture I get of the room, though, the more worried I am. It is not quite what I would call filth—not like Wilson's place gets when his parents are away—but it has a lonely quality to it. This is how I imagine a room would look if someone's life stopped abruptly, but the mail kept accumulating with no one there to organize it, even to throw it away.

Wilson, after having his own hesitations out on the porch, is now in full gear. He sits down and leans back into the cushion of the chair, smacking its arms with his hands and crossing his legs in an exaggerated pose of comfort.

"So, Mr. Roverson, what you been doing with yourself?" He adds the *Mr.* this time, but his words still drip with disrespect.

"I've kept myself busy. All these papers here are for my job."

"You got a job?" Wilson asks.

"I still have to pay bills, Wilson. It's not much. A little Internet work. I solicit potential customers for architecture magazines, and if I get a lead I follow up via regular mail. That's what you see all around you."

Wilson looks around, nodding, seeming to take inventory of the room. After my first glances at the disarray, I've preferred to keep my eyes glued on Wilson and to take cues from him.

Roverson disappears for a minute and calls to us from the kitchen, asking if we want anything to drink.

"Whiskey," Wilson calls.

"Not funny, Wilson. I have orange juice, water, or milk."

We don't answer. Instead, I lean over to Wilson and tell him it's high time we got out of this place.

"You've got no balls, Gary. Let's see what this guy has on his mind. He clearly wanted us in here for a reason. The least we could do is find out."

"Bullshit, Wilson. This is creeping me out. This guy's lost it."

"Okay, but let me ask him about Lindy first."

That notion keeps me held for a while. I wonder if maybe, just maybe, Roverson would be willing to talk about her. Talk about what they did, how they did it, when and where. When it comes to sex, I'm starved for details.

Roverson comes back in with two glasses of water, even

though we didn't ask for any. He clears off two spots on the coffee table in front of us and sets the drinks down, the glasses beading with water onto the wood. I look for a coaster, but when I see the marks, cuts, and stains on the wood, I know it doesn't matter to Roverson what happens to his coffee table.

Wilson takes a sip and looks straight at Roverson, smiling. I know this look on Wilson, the devilish grin that's ready to test somebody's will.

"So, Mr. Roverson. You talk to your honey lately?"

Roverson just narrows his eyes at Wilson, not answering.

"Lindy," Wilson continues. "You talk to Lindy since she went public?"

Leave it to Wilson to go right for the jugular, to throw a lit match on a pool of gasoline. I expect an outburst from Roverson, a tirade that would put my dad to shame, but just as I start to flinch in anticipation of it, I see that Roverson takes the question calmly. He sighs and looks away, but doesn't show even the slightest anger. Not a reaction I'm used to.

"You have a direct way, don't you, Wilson?" he says.

"If that means I want to know the dirt on you and Lindy, yes." He smiles again, like he's just played a winning card. And again, Roverson doesn't bite.

"Don't you two read the papers? Watch the news? Lord, there's nothing I could tell you that hasn't been exaggerated a thousand times over in every corner of this spiteful little town."

Half of me is a little disappointed that Roverson isn't up for divulging any dirty secrets, but the other half of me hopes that will be the end of it, and that we can make a quick exit. Wilson, of course, isn't about to let go that easy.

"It's just that when I talked to Lindy," he says, "she didn't seem to think it was as big a deal as everyone was making it out to be."

Finally, Roverson gives a visible reaction, his chin snapping up as he inhales sharply. He stands up and takes a few strides across the room, his back to us, his head hung down in his hand. Three separate times he takes a breath as if to speak, but then hesitates, like he's thought better of his words. I reach over and tug on Wilson's shirt, jerk my thumb to the door. Wilson, though, just slaps my hand away and points to Roverson. He bulges his eyes as me, a signal for me to hold tight for just a little longer.

Roverson turns back to us and sits down again, smiles.

"You know Lindy?" he asks. His face is calm, but there is a small quiver in his voice, and for the first time he seems on the defensive. When he asks this he leans forward, but then straightens back up, smoothes the front of his shirt nervously across his broad chest.

"Sure," Wilson answers. "Who the hell you think told me you kept your spare keys in your glove compartment?"

Roverson clears his throat.

"When did you see her last?"

"Right before her parents sent her packing up to Hammond."

Roverson rubs his hands together and then laces his fingers in his lap, like he's trying to will them into stillness.

"And she didn't seem to think what happened between us was a . . . a big deal?" he asks.

"Well, I don't know if she said that," Wilson answers. I can tell by the grin on his face, by the glimmer in his eyes, that Wilson's enjoying this strange power he has over Roverson's attention. "I just don't think she understood why the town made such a big deal about it."

"Nor do I," Roverson mutters. "Some of those bastards at school would have you believe I killed someone."

To me, though, it *is* a big deal. Sex between anyone I know seems huge, but the way Roverson shrugs it off, I'm starting to wonder if anything happened between them at all. I can restrain my curiosity no longer and clear my throat. Both Roverson and Wilson look at me as if they'd forgotten I was there with them.

"So did you two? You know."

"Of course, Gary," Roverson says. "And I don't claim to be proud of it. Neither am I as ashamed as this lousy town wants me to be."

Again, I feel locked out of important knowledge. It isn't enough to know that Roverson and Lindy had sex, I want to know details. How it started, how many times it happened, how it *felt*. But again, I don't have the courage to ask any more questions.

Instead, Wilson turns the conversation again, prodding Roverson about use of the car. I shrink back into my chair and sip my water, feeling like a completely unnecessary part of Wilson's endeavors, like I'm just some shadow that follows him as he walks and lives in the light.

After some hesitation, Roverson digs the keys to the Lincoln from his pockets and dangles them in front of us, preparing to drop them into Wilson's waiting palm. Before he turns them over, though, he decides to give us a few instructions. He stands and motions his hand toward the clutter of the room.

"You can see, I'm sure, that things here have slipped a bit," he says.

"That's putting it nicely," Wilson pops.

"Wilson, your smart mouth will get you in trouble someday. One might think that since I'm giving you free rein to my car, you'd treat me with some respect. In fact, I'm going to ask more than that. I want you boys to help out around here now and then, with tidying the place up and helping me with these mail orders. Three sets of hands could increase my income, and your share would be use of the car—with some restrictions, of course. What do you say?"

Wilson hesitates and purses his lips, pondering the option presented to us. He has his hand outstretched under the dangling keys. Then he snatches them from Roverson as quick as a cat pouncing on a bird.

"Whatever, boss," Wilson says.

Roverson follows us to the door and then darts in front of us before we can exit. He tells us that this whole arrangement, of course, must be kept in secrecy. It has to be that way, he explains, because it's illegal for us to be driving his car, and he doesn't want the town knowing any more of his dealings than they already do.

"If it weren't for the prying of a bored, small town, things would still be just fine for me," he says.

I look up at him, his massive frame. He is simultaneously a model of fitness and a man fallen. He carries an adult-sized grudge against the town in the same way I'm frustrated by it in adolescence. And he's made it further sexually with a student of Dearborn Springs High School than I have. Roverson, I realize, is in many ways as much a peer as he is an adult, and something inside me starts craving his approval. Dammit, I want him to like me. And I want him to teach me what he knows.

Wilson is already bounding down the drive, the crunch of his feet in the gravel breaking the slow rhythm of the hot night. I turn back to Roverson and thank him.

"Don't mention it, Gary. It's better than you two sneaking around here. You could have gotten hurt that way."

He reaches out and shakes my hand, giving it a firm pump. Despite his sorrowful eyes, his body still carries a strength, and his hand gripping mine seems to lend some of the strength to me. I can feel my chest swell with it.

"I hope we can make it up to you, Mr. Roverson," I say.

He keeps my hand in his and gives it another hearty pump. "Don't worry," he says. "I'm sure we'll find a way to even everything up."

I start down the drive, and I can see Wilson settling in behind the wheel, rolling down the window to let his arm dangle out. He's looking down at his lap like he's searching for something, and I know he's digging out a smoke.

"Gary," Roverson calls. I turn around and he continues, "I know you're the reasonable one between you and Wilson, so use some sense, okay? I know Wilson is hell-bent on causing whatever trouble he can. I'm trusting you to keep things under control. And under wraps."

"You got it," I call back.

In the passenger seat next to Wilson, I feel as powerful as if I were the one driving: Roverson trusts *me*. It makes me feel slightly high, even this small suggestion of his approval. Wilson hands me a smoke, which I take, beaming out a smile.

"What are you so giddy about, kid?" he asks.

"Nothing," I say.

"Spill it."

"Oh, I was just thinking about Roverson nailing Lindy," I lie. "How lucky that prick is."

"Shit. Lindy ain't all that good. Trust me."

We start down the road, rolling toward town in the muggy, dusty night. The subject of Lindy won't seem to extinguish in my head now that I've brought it up again.

"Did Lindy really say it wasn't that big of a deal?" I ask.

"Shit, Gary. She barely talked about it. I was just making most of that up to fuck with Roverson. You see his eyes when I mentioned her? Funny as hell."

He drives on, laughing at his own words. He flips on the radio and starts to sing along with Axl Rose, who's screaming over the static. In the rearview mirror, I can see Roverson's house shrinking, and across the lane, the other farmhouses are disappearing. I think of Lindy and Wilson, and wonder how she could possibly not measure up, not be *all that good*. Nevertheless, I feel like Wilson's claims are growing a bit transparent, and that the pact we sealed with Roverson is as real as anything I could wish for. Before we walked in that door I wanted nothing to do with him, but now I see good possibilities in Roverson. I can almost taste the change on the air.

Chapter 8

"**I** thought the guy was gonna be cool," Wilson says.

We're at Roverson's again, and already we've worked out a rhythm. Wilson and I go to work, mostly on a seemingly endless pile of envelopes—organizing them into stacks for Roverson, or stuffing them with form letters. Occasionally, he has us help clean in other ways, but mostly it's just paper shuffling. We do that for an hour or so, and then Roverson hands us the keys, always attaching orders Wilson disregards at will: no passengers, no leaving town, no drinking.

This is the third time we've done the exchange, and already Wilson is growing bored with it—the hour of chores must seem like a lifetime to him.

I look at him and shrug, say it's not that bad a deal.

"I don't mind the work," he says.

"Liar," I tease.

"Okay. I mind it. But not as much as I mind him nosing around. Really, I thought the guy was cooler than this—I mean, he did nail Lindy after all."

I don't understand why it bothers Wilson so much. Roverson is not so overbearing, if you ask me. Sure, he checks up on what we're doing, chats with us some, but it's more being friendly than anything else.

Wilson calls to Roverson, who's out in the kitchen. "Hey, Mr. Roverson. You got those keys ready? Gary and I are gonna split."

Roverson walks into the living room, looking at us but not answering. He brings his wrist up to his eyes, like a military motion. Already he's regained some of the precision I used to associate with him.

"Why, Wilson," he says, "unless my eyes deceive, you've been here less than half an hour. Don't tell me you are so thin on patience that you can't complete a few simple tasks before you get antsy."

Wilson huffs and stands, growing visibly impatient.

"Come on, man. Give us a break for once."

Roverson sits on his couch, smiling. He unclasps his watch and sets it on the table in front of him, making a production of it.

"You two," he says. "Let me tell you something."

I see Wilson roll his eyes, and I can almost hear him thinking, *Not another lecture.* Thing is, when Roverson comes out to talk to us, I kind of enjoy it. He's proven to be worthy of a few insights so far, and he has a nice, patient tone with us that I'm not used to from adults.

"You can't go and get yourself in a hurry. It's a sure way to get yourself in a predicament, one big damn fix."

He narrows his eyes when he says *damn*, like he's conspiring with us. Wilson snorts, but I lean in, listening.

Roverson picks up on Wilson's disgust and says, "Let me remind you, young Mr. England, that I could still call the police on you for stealing my car. So before you act like you know everything, just remember that."

"Wouldn't stick," Wilson says. "Besides, you can't call the cops on me for something I did weeks ago."

"Oh, no? I suppose you have a law degree, Wilson. I suppose you know everything. Well, we'll just see." He picks up the phone, starts to dial deliberately.

I elbow Wilson. He might be bluffing, but I don't really want to find out. Wilson makes a pained face at me, but finally relents and asks Roverson to put the phone down.

Roverson smiles, puts the phone back in its cradle.

"Look, boys. All I'm saying is that you can't be looking for a quick fix. Shoot, the deal I've given you two is the closest thing there is to a shortcut . . . and still that's not good enough for you."

"I'm not complaining," I say. "I just wish we had more to do than stuff envelopes."

Wilson turns his head to me when I say it, jaw out with a slight sense of betrayal.

"Interesting, Gary," Roverson says. "You want more responsibility? Now that is a good sign. You're proving to be responsible so far, and that's the best way for you to get something out of this."

He emphasises the *you* and *you're* to me, obviously contrasting me with Wilson. I can sense Wilson's impatience growing, almost like there's a heat coming off him.

"Let me ask you one thing," Wilson says. "If you're so wise, how come you got in *one big damn fix* with Lindy? Huh? Tell us that."

Roverson smiles, like he was waiting for this question. "Well, maybe you can learn from my mistakes. But let me tell you this"—he leans toward us for emphasis, looking first at Wilson and then directly at me—"don't think you know everything about what happened between me and Lindy. Give me that much credit."

With that, he nods at us, stands, and walks back toward the kitchen. His watch is still sitting on the table and he calls back without looking, "Don't think about asking for the keys again until that watch says six-thirty."

We start back into the pile of envelopes, Wilson shaking his head.

"He always does that," he says.

"What?"

"Brings up Lindy just for a second and then drops it. I don't know what the hell he's trying to prove. Like he's teasing us."

It's barely 10:30 and Marny is already after Frank. Like the fool he is, he forgot to add milk to the ice-cream maker, and now we're behind schedule, with the first customers rolling in. I'm feeling distant, too—my thoughts always seem to be on Roverson, the way he seems interested in me and Wilson and then just kind of drops hints about Lindy. If nothing else, it adds flavor to what would otherwise be a dull summer day.

"Frank, that's about as simple as breathing," Marny says. She can get cruel when she wants.

"But, Mrs. Lydle. Gary said . . ."

"Stop. Just stop. Don't blame that on Gary. Look at the job

chart and whose name does it say? It says Frank. Blaming it on someone else is almost as bad as not doing the job."

She keeps after him like this, following him around the kitchen, her words chasing him past the syrup canisters, the blenders, the walk-in.

I've seen her get like this with other workers, not just Frank. I remember coming in here other summers when Wilson and I would ride over for milk shakes and tacos. Always Marny or Mr. Lydle would have the workers rolling their eyes in disgust, red-faced at being called out in front of the customers. I remember a girl three or four years older than us, Leah, was on the wrong end of one of Mr. Lydle's lectures. Wilson and I stood on the other side of the window, waiting for our order, watching Leah's eyes get red and moist until the tears started to flow. Within minutes she was storming back toward the kitchen, head hung low, and then we saw her through the window as she raced across the parking lot, her face buried in her hands. Lydle just turned back to us like nothing had happened and handed us our milk shakes.

It figures that two years later, I'd be spending my summer on the other side of the glass, taking those same orders and ducking the anger of the Lydles. At least I'm not in Frank's shoes. It's strange how I struggle to figure anything out but, when next to Frank, I can always see his mistakes and what he should do differently. I wonder if that's how Wilson feels sometimes when he's around me—like he can see the way out from under my father's pressure, or how to make things work with Lauryn. And even though I'm getting the hang of my job, it's still a loser's task compared to Wilson's. He's always talking about getting to work outside on the paint crew, and how the older guys will hook him up with beers on breaks.

Maybe the hard work here prepares me better for the chores at Roverson's. At least there, Roverson talks to us like a reasonable person instead of yelling at us like Lydle. The last time we were over, Wilson got impatient—again. Roverson, instead of threatening to call the cops, just said we could call the whole thing off. I thought Wilson was going to take him up on it, so I piped up fast and said we were still up for it if Roverson was.

Later, when Wilson was off in the bathroom, Roverson talked just to me. He knew from seeing me at school that I was seeing Lauryn, and he also detected that it wasn't always easy with her. "You're a good kid, Gary," he said. "You're helpful, intelligent, you pay attention. I'm sure she sees that in you, so just don't push the other stuff. Just control what you can—and you might realize that's more than you thought."

Mr. Lydle is up at the order window, and we're already starting to get busy. The summer has ratcheted up the heat on Dearborn Springs, which is good business for the Dairy Castle. The fake ice-cream cone spinning outside somehow looks more appetizing when the temperature climbs over ninety.

"Gary!" he calls. "Get your bones up here."

I walk up to the front and he stands over me, sweating. The man is overweight and constantly panting and sweating. I've started to worry that someday he'll drop in the middle of fixing an ice-cream soda. The sad part is that I'm not as concerned about his health as I am the notion that, between Marny and Frank, I'd have to be the voice of reason in crisis.

"Look, son. Those two are at it again, and neither one of them has enough sense to come up and help me here on the line. I'm caught up on taking the orders, so try to get the ice cream out and I'll go talk to them."

My specialty is back with the food, handling the tacos, burritos, and nachos. I dread handling the ice-cream orders alone, because that's what gets the Lydles the most aggravated when something goes wrong. I look out and see the faces of the customers, all eyes staring back impatiently. I don't recognize any of them—they're all older, either housewives or older guys on break from work. Still, I get the sense that they all somehow know me, that any misstep will be noticed.

Lydle starts stomping past the row of ice-cream tubs, past the food line and into the kitchen. Before he gets to Marny, who's still lecturing Frank back by the sink, I call to him and ask what to do if someone comes in for an order. He never lets us handle the money.

"Just write down what they want, and I'll come handle their cash in a few minutes! Geez, do I have to hold your hand up there?"

His tone makes me nervous, and I'm certain all the people waiting for their food heard it. His grumbling diminishes as he heads toward the clamor of Marny and Frank, and my eyes focus on the tickets lined up on the counter. There are so many of them, it's intimidating.

I pause and think about what Roverson's told me. So I take things one step at a time like Roverson would say. Grabbing the scooper, I start to dish up the first sundae. I glance back at the length of tickets, and they seem like days lined up across a calendar, each one looking just like the next—but I know I can get through it.

I even hinted to Roverson last time that things were beyond

my control at home. He said that's always beyond a teenager's control, but when I didn't say anything in return, he must have sensed that it was worse than I was letting on.

"Gary, a lot of kids have it rough at home," he said. "Lindy was that way, too."

"I didn't know that. What was wrong there?" I asked, wanting to change the subject.

"That doesn't matter, Gary. Just remember that if you need help you can ask. We're getting to be friends, and friends can ask for each other's help, right?"

I nodded.

"Just remember not to get too far ahead of yourself. Stay focused on what's right in front of you."

Now, arm halfway into the chill of the ice-cream bin, digging hard for a scoop from a frozen bucket of vanilla, I start to think of how many days there are like this in front of me. Not just at the Dairy Castle, digging for ice cream under the unblinking stare of the customers—and there are plenty of these days left in this summer—but in my future here in Dearborn Springs. There are at least three years left of high school. Then what? College somewhere else? Even I know that I have to get myself in gear if I want that to happen. If not that, then a job here in town? Another restaurant? One of the auto plants?

None of the options seem real, and certainly not acceptable. Moreover, in all those cloudy images of the future, there are two things missing from the picture: Wilson and Lauryn. I get the sense that they'll find a way out no matter what. Lauryn will go to college somewhere, and Wilson is simply too big for this town to hold—even if his dad's job doesn't take him away, something else will. I might be able to take these orders one step at a time, but my future is a different challenge altogether.

I finally dig through the orders and get them out the door, the customers all satisfied enough to stop staring at me. Luckily, nobody else has come in for an order, but I know it won't be long until we're swamped again with the early lunch crowd.

Mr. Lydle comes out front, mopping his head with a handkerchief.

"Goddamn kid is gonna be the death of me. I mean, I've been here many a summer, and I don't know if I've seen a kid that inept."

I ask him if he's going to hang on to him, or if I should still scout for potential employees to help finish the summer. There's a glimmer of hope in me that thinks maybe I could get Wilson on here to liven up the rest of my summer work, even though I know he wouldn't give up his job on the paint crew. Lydle just grumbles anyway, not really answering. Then he growls, "Well, goddamn. This day can't get any finer."

"What?" I ask. But then I follow his gaze and see what he has to blame his mood on today: the Lincoln again, rolling into the parking lot, the heat rising in little waves over its black hood.

"Roverson," I say under my breath.

"Damn if it isn't. Guy barely shows his face in town and now he comes to my business twice this summer."

"You want me to take his order?" I ask Lydle.

"You sound like you're eager to talk to the guy," Lydle says. His chest heaving, splotches of sweat coming out under his armpits and at his belly, Lydle stares down at me disapprovingly.

"No," I sputter. "I just remember last time you didn't seem

to want to talk to him. I figured, if you let me take his order you wouldn't have to talk to him at all."

"You're right," he says, then pauses and stares at me again. "Not that I really want to deal with half the fools in this town, but Roverson is even worse than most. You call back what he orders to me and I'll holler the price up to you. Got it?"

I nod, and Lydle disappears back into the kitchen again. His disgust for Roverson bothers me, but then Lydle seems disgusted by just about everyone. Even if customers take a minute to decide what they want to order, he'll get huffy and irritated. I look back and see that at least Marny has stopped harassing Frank long enough for both of them to get back to work: Marny cleaning pots and pans and Frank preparing taco meat.

The door swings open and there's Roverson—as much as his spirits and appearances have rebounded at his house, he seems nervous to be in town. He gives a quick smile of recognition to me and it breaks the cloud that seems to hang over him.

The attention of the customers lifts from their food to Roverson, and they stare at him just as intently as I felt they did when Lydle scolded me. Abruptly, one woman swings her child out of the booth, cradles the remainder of her food in the crook of her elbow, and exits, eyes glaring at Roverson all the time. I wonder if that's why Roverson doesn't go into town much, because he can always feel the eyes on him whenever he walks through a door. I feel sorry for him when I see that. If only people knew what he's really like.

He steps up to the counter and orders a taco mild, a scoop of strawberry, and a medium Coke. I echo the order to Lydle and he calls back to me with a gruff *four-fifteen*.

Roverson smiles at me again and slides a ten my way. I shove the change back across the counter, but he pulls his hand away from it.

"No, Gary," he says. He talks low so nobody else can hear. "That's for you. Consider it an incentive for keeping Wilson in line with my car, and for all the help you've given me around the house."

I've earned heftier chunks of change. Still, I appreciate the notion.

"Thanks," I say, keeping my voice as low as his. We don't even look at each other when we speak, like the smallest gesture might tip off everything.

"You got a second, Gary?"

I look back to the kitchen and see that everyone else is absorbed in their work, paying no attention to me.

"Not long," I say. I pull the tub of strawberry from the freezer and bring it up to the counter, so I can fix his cone as we talk.

"You and Wilson share just about everything, don't you?" Roverson starts. "I mean, there aren't many secrets between you two."

I could tell Roverson that there are secrets Wilson keeps from me: where he disappears to sometimes, why he turns sullen and angry for no apparent reason. Or I could tell Roverson that half of what Wilson tells me is probably a lie anyway, but that I choose to latch onto every word like the most precious of secrets. I could tell Roverson all this and more, but the only word that can make its way out of my mouth is a muffled *sure*.

Roverson gives a short, breathy laugh and then leans toward me, his elbows on the counter, his head almost completely through the pickup window.

"What I'm getting at, Gary, is I wonder if you *could* keep a secret from Wilson."

This suggestion stops me cold. It never crossed my mind that there might be something I'd know that Wilson wouldn't. Roverson has an earnest look on his face, his eyes now intent and full of life.

"I don't know. I've never been asked to before."

"Gary," he says. He puts his hand flat on the counter like he's testifying. "I need someone I can trust, and I don't think Wilson can be the person. It's got to be you for this one thing."

"What is it?"

"There's not enough time to explain that now. Can you come out tonight, but without Wilson along?"

My curiosity is boiling over. I can't imagine what I could help Roverson with, but there's a strange tinge of pride from being asked for the favor, whatever it may be. I remember, though, that I'm meeting Lauryn after work, and I want to spend this evening trying to make things right with her.

"Can I come by tomorrow night instead?" I ask.

"Sure. Sooner is better, but tomorrow night will do."

We agree on it, set the time for 8:30 tomorrow night. I look around to make sure that nobody is eyeing us suspiciously, and then I go fix Roverson his taco and Coke. His secrecy is killing me, and as I fix the rest of his order I search for something I could help him with. I'm blank on it, though.

I get him his food and, without saying another word, he backs out the door like he did before. There's no wink this time, though. Just a solemn and meaningful nod of his head.

Lydle shuffles back to the front, with Marny and Frank trailing behind him.

"Sonofabitch gone?" Lydle asks.

I tell him he left without a word. Lydle harumphs and leans on the counter, watching Roverson's Lincoln exit the parking lot, waiting for his lunch customers to come rolling in.

"Frank," Marny creaks, "did you get enough hot dogs for all the coneys we'll sell at lunch? We're just now caught up, and we can't afford to get backed up during the lunch rush."

"Yeah, I—" Frank starts. "I think there are enough. How many do we need?"

I can tell by the doubt in his voice that he has no clue and that he's entirely unprepared for the onslaught we'll get in about fifteen minutes. It frustrates me as much as it does the Lydles at this point—we're almost halfway through the summer, and Frank still can't get things straight.

This kitchen—one can't remember more than two orders at a time, one can't remember my name, and one can't go ten paces without breaking out in a sweat. And then there's me, who now has a little more responsibility thrust on me than I'm used to.

I start helping Frank, and I give him instructions in soothing tones, trying to calm his nerves. In his hands, though, everything is a crisis about to happen. He picks up hot pans with no gloves, drops pots full of food, and knocks over anything within a three-foot radius of his awkward body.

With him, it's one step forward and two back. My life, it seems, has been like that this summer—moving in a hurry but getting nowhere fast. I wonder which direction my steps with Roverson will lead me in.

Chapter 9

Lauryn isn't in the most talkative mood. She's still a bit hot over our fight at her house, even though it was more than a week ago. It took some pleading to even get her to meet me here. Every time I mess up with her, it gets a little tougher to talk her into giving me another chance. Just like my unused sexual energy is mounting in me, her frustrations with me accumulate, too. I fear that soon, that's all we'll be—just frustrations slamming into each other.

Now she sits across from me and sips on her chocolate malt. She flips the top off and alternates between spoon and straw, staring down into it like she's deep in thought. Fresh off my shift and plowing through my free meal—a heaping plate of nachos with extra meat, peppers, sour cream, and cheese—I'm sure I don't look my best for her. My hair is all messed up, and my T-shirt is splotched with food scraps that my apron didn't catch.

"When you pressure me it just makes me back off further," she says.

"I know that."

"Then if you know why do you keep pressuring?"

It's a valid question. More than that, it seems to be *the* question between us, one that needs to be addressed more than anything. Only I don't have an answer for it. When I step back from us and look, I can almost slow myself down enough so things work between us. But as soon as I let go, as soon as I lose sight of a long view between us, I want everything right now. When I get like that, it feels like there is no other moment with her than the present.

"I'm sorry," I say.

Lauryn stirs her malt. "You know what your problem is?" she says. "You think the world is like Wilson makes it."

I give a big sigh when she brings up Wilson. When she gets to lecturing me about Wilson, about how it's doing me no good to hang out with him, she's as bad as my mother trying to give me a lecture on school work.

"Why do you always have to bad-mouth Wilson? He's my best friend."

I burst out with that and then remember that I'm still supposed to be in apology mode, so I reach over to take her fingers in my hand and add: "Well, you're my best friend, Lauryn. I mean he's my best *guy* friend."

Lauryn yanks her hand away and shoves her index finger in her mouth, makes a sound like she's wretching. Removing her finger, she lets her face break into a big, full smile. Then she starts laughing. I, in turn, pretend to be offended.

"I'm glad you find me so amusing, Lauryn. You take compliments *so* well."

"Oh, come off it, Gary. Don't even."

I start laughing then, too. This is why I am so wrapped up in her, how she can light up a day and make me take things less seriously. She starts back in on Wilson, but I take it this time, the laugh we shared making even this subject easy to tackle.

Lauryn says it's not that she doesn't like Wilson, it's that she doesn't like how easily I follow him. After I've been around him it's like I'm a completely different person, she says, not the one she likes, not the one she wants to have as a boyfriend.

"It's this town," I say. "Living here, in Dearborn Springs, under my roof. Damn. It just drives me nuts. If it weren't for Wilson, I'd have gone crazy by now."

She shrugs and says, "I think it's just the opposite, crazy boy. I *like* how you want out of this town. I just don't like that you think you can get out by following Wilson."

She seems so assured, so solid in her beliefs, that I know I can't win. In many ways, she's right. Sometimes it's like I don't have a will of my own, so I have to borrow strength from others. It's not just Wilson, though. It's Lauryn, too. And now Roverson.

Looking at her like that, her back erect against the back of the booth, I know the best I can hope for is compromise.

"Well, I'm not going to stop hanging out with Wilson, but I do want to make things right with you. Look, I'll think about what you're saying. And I'll . . . I'll watch myself. I won't just follow Wilson without thinking."

As I say it, I know I probably won't have the strength to do it. But I want to change for her, and wanting seems like the most important thing right now.

The whole time, customers shuffle in and out, floating past us. The next shift has come on; Frank and I are free to roam the rest of the summer day. The Lydles are still at it, though, working hard. Every once in a while, Mr. Lydle will arrange for his daughter to come in and run the place, but the rest of the time he is there behind that window, taking orders at all hours of the day. At least they shut down for the winter, but it is a tough schedule they set up for themselves.

Marny comes out to wipe down the tables, humming to herself the whole time. Sometimes she pauses, raises her hand to her chin as if she's forgotten why she's standing there, rag in hand. She looks at me with vague comprehension, like she can't quite place me even though I was working with her in the kitchen less than twenty minutes ago.

"Jerry, er, Gary," she says. She comes to our table and smiles at us as she wipes it down around our food.

"Hi, Marny. This is Lauryn."

Lauryn extends her hand to Marny and gives her a broad smile.

"Are you Gary's girlfriend?" Marny asks.

Lauryn gives a small giggle, but answers yes. Marny shakes her hand vigorously at that news and puts her arm around Lauryn's shoulder in a small hug. Lauryn looks at me, a bit surprised by the level of affection Marny is showing.

"This boy," Marny says. "This boy is a find. He's not like some of the other kids we get around here, like that Frank. Gary is a good kid. He handles whatever we throw at him, he even handled that Roverson character today. You hang on to this kid."

Lauryn laughs, looking at me again. I can see a blush rising under her dark complexion, and although I'd like an endorsement from a more reliable source, I appreciate Marny talking me up to Lauryn. I can use all the help I can get.

Marny proceeds to corner Lauryn in a conversation, taking a break she'd surely jump me or Frank for. One time Frank got in trouble for walking outside for ten minutes to talk to his *mother*. But now, Marny takes the time to inquire about Lauryn's parents, her grades, her summer, her plans. After a while, Lauryn becomes absorbed in the conversation and has Marny telling stories about her own children and grandchildren.

Before long, a line of customers extends out the door. When she notices, Marny quickly excuses herself, stumbling over both of our names as she leaves.

Lauryn and I turn back to our food, both of us finishing up. I talk Lauryn into coming back to my house just to watch television, but first I have to promise that I have nothing up my sleeve, that at least one of my parents will be home, and I won't try to get her to do anything she doesn't want to.

Before we go, though, Lauryn asks what Marny meant by me handling Roverson. Lauryn mentioning his name catches me off guard, and for a second I feel like she's discovered our entire operation—the car theft, the joyrides, the visits to Roverson himself.

"What?" I ask.

"She said it right when she got to our table. She said you 'handled Roverson.'"

"Oh. Mr. Lydle didn't want to talk to him, got all worked up. So I took his order instead."

Lauryn's face pinches in an expression of disapproval, her eyebrows pointing down.

"Roverson," she says, spitting out the name. "That man. I don't blame Mr. Lydle for not wanting to talk to that . . . that asshole."

Lauryn does not use obscenity lightly, so I know she must truly despise Roverson. Not that I expected Lauryn to be in his corner, but I'm surprised to hear this much anger in her voice.

"That's a pretty strong word, don't you think?"

"What? Gary, there aren't strong enough words to describe that man."

I don't want to start another argument with Lauryn, but I don't think the guy seems that bad. If anything, he seems saddened by the whole ordeal.

"Look, I'm not trying to say Roverson didn't do anything. But is it that horrible?"

"Gary!" she says, her voice really carrying now, enough to turn the heads of a few other customers. Then she drops it back into a hush to finish. "You don't think *rape* is that horrible?"

"Rape? Jesus, Lauryn. Lindy was completely willing. Nobody's ever disputed that."

Lauryn's anger is growing, I can see it in her eyes. Still, she keeps her voice calm.

"When it's a teacher and a student it can't be anything but rape, Gary. It's all about power. And that dirty man used his power to rape that girl, whether she *thought* she wanted to or not."

It strikes me that she's giving Lindy a little less credit than she deserves, like she was completely without control over her own actions. I mean, she *was* eighteen. I know enough to stop arguing though, and I try to distance myself from Roverson.

"Look, Lauryn. Let's just go. I don't want to fight again, especially not over a guy as useless as Roverson."

"Agreed," she says.

We stand to leave and start on the fifteen-minute walk to my house. As soon as we're out the door, the heat and humidity descend on us. Immediately, I can feel my sweat gathering around my neck and arms, and I can't remember a summer that has carried this kind of heat, this kind of constant pressure.

Three-thirty in the afternoon, and my dad already has five empty beer cans on the end table next to him. He's presiding over the remote, and Lauryn and I are on the couch, silently watching him flip.

In this house, even the way he changes channels can be violent.

Flip, flip, flip, and he settles on CNN. He mutters something about job cuts and the know-it-all talking heads.

Flip, flip, flip, and he settles on a science fiction show. He mutters again, only the words "what shit" audible.

Flip, flip, and he settles on a music video, a hip-hop group out on the beach. He grumbles that we'd probably like that, but he looks only at Lauryn when he says it.

He goes on like this seemingly without end, and I keep hoping that he'll just stop on something, anything, so we can focus on the television instead of my horrible father. Lauryn leans toward me and whispers a suggestion for popping in a movie.

"Dad," I say. No answer.

When I first started up with Lauryn, I delayed for months before I invited her over. Hanging at her house was always much safer: Her parents pried, but at least they weren't like my dad. My mom kept insisting that I invite Lauryn over, though—*You mention this girl enough*, she said, *I think it's high time we meet her*. I tried to pick a time when my dad would be out, but it didn't work, he was there waiting when Lauryn came over, waiting to play judge. He tried to act pleasant in anticipation, but as soon as he saw her he started frowning and then he decided just to ignore her. My mom sat us down in the living room and made small talk, my dad shuffling through wordlessly every once in a while, on his way to the kitchen or the garage, looking right through us like we were ghosts. Finally, when she was leaving she called out to my dad that it was nice to meet him, he called back, *Yeah, a thrill*, the first words he'd said in an hour and a half.

I apologized for him, told her how embarrassed I was by him, by everything in that house. Lauryn seemed untroubled by it, though. She said she could *see right through his act*. She's caught more of his silent treatment than she ever has his outward anger, but she's seen enough of him to know. Still, every time she comes over I feel shame wash over me, and I want everything to be different—if not for my sake, then for hers.

I call to my dad again, trying to get the remote from him, but still get no answer. And, just like that, I've had it. Roverson may think patience is all I need, but he's never met my father. I'm sick of his bullying and his raging and his control. It's bad enough that he does it to me and Mom, but acting this way in front of my girlfriend is too much. I stand up and walk toward him, determined to show both my father and Lauryn that I won't be pushed around so easily.

As I move toward him, he doesn't budge. He's got his chin buried in his chest, the fat at his neck bulging out, and his arm lying on his knee, the remote hanging loosely in his hand. His whole body rises and falls with each breath, and he looks like he could be sleeping.

I reach down and snatch the remote from his fingers. His head jerks up when I do it. Immediately, I turn back to the couch, giving a quick wink of confidence toward Lauryn. Only she doesn't return that look of confidence—her face is alarmed. Without seeing him, I know my father is at my back, ready to do damage. I don't hear him, but I hear the chair rock back, released from his weight.

I try to turn, but it's too late. Both his hands hit my shoulders, and I fall into the couch beside Lauryn. It wasn't enough to hurt physically, but my pride is shattered. I'm torn between wanting to kill him and simply wanting to curl up and cry.

Hands on his hips, like he's proud of himself, he stands there and stares down at the two of us. On my thigh, I feel Lauryn's fingers—an attempt to bring calm to me. I brush those fingers aside with my left hand, and with my right I fling the remote back at my father. It bounces off the cushion of his belly and falls to the floor.

"Pick it up and hand it to me."

"You weren't watching anything. Dammit, I just want to throw in a movie."

He clears his throat.

"Pick it up," he says more deliberately, "and hand it to me."

I sit there, not looking at him. My vision falls on the floor, where the remote lies. I feel like if I can just focus on that, on that innocent rectangle of black on the dirty cream-colored carpet, all the rest will go away: my father, his noise, even Lauryn. Right now I want everything to be gone.

In that line of vision, I see Lauryn's hand creeping toward

the remote, inching toward it carefully. She gingerly picks it up and hands it to my father.

"No," he says.

Lauryn looks up at him wordlessly—he's got an anger in his voice usually reserved for me and my mom, and to have it issued in her direction has her scared.

"Put it back down," he continues.

Lauryn stands there in front of him, frozen. I should act, do something to stand up for her, but I know if I move I'll just get knocked back down.

My father keeps speaking, overemphasizing each word in a mocking tone more fitting for one of a bullying classmate.

"Are you deaf, girl?" he says. "I told you to put the remote down. I want you to put it down so my son can pick it back up and hand it to me in a respectful manner. Do you understand, or do I need to draw you a picture?"

Lauryn whimpers out, "I understand," and bends gently down to replace the remote on its spot on the floor. As soon as she does, my father starts at me again, instructing me to pick it up like he said. Anything, I would give anything to be able to stand up to him. Only a minute ago I had the courage to walk across the room and yank the remote out of his hand, but now I feel as if my legs have lost their ability to function.

He cuffs me once on the back of the head and that gets my body in motion. I lean down, pick up the remote—all this over a stupid remote—and hand it to him, completing the humiliation.

Without a word, he goes back to his chair and begins it all again—*flip, flip, flip.*

I take Lauryn's hand and lead her from the couch. We walk

outside and sit on the front stoop. In front of us, the lawn is brown and dying, weeds sticking up like miniature tombstones. It is exactly how I feel inside — burned and choked.

"I'm sorry," I say.

Lauryn wraps herself around my right arm and squeezes. The warmth in her arms brings me back into reality. At some point I sank inside of myself and was just watching what was going on, like I was a character I was watching on television. Her touch, her voice, always balance me.

"Gary," she says, "you don't have to apologize to me. Not for that. Never for that."

I can't help but be filled with shame, though, and I tell her that I should have done something. The apologies keep spilling out of me, until she stops them with the smallest, quickest of kisses. When her lips touch mine, it stops everything inside me that wants to race away, that wants to change the world all at once. I realize that this is why I'm with her, why I want so much to do right by her: She's the one I can depend on when everything else is falling apart. Wilson might pick me up with levity, have the guts to talk back to my dad, but Lauryn is more sincere in her support, and her connection to me sometimes feels like it's part of my core. Her kisses, her touches, those are the things I want. But her company is what I need. I just wish I could remember this all the time.

"Thank you," I say.

We start walking back toward her house. On the way, she reassures me that there's nothing I can do about a man twice my size acting like a child half my age. Every time I start to raise doubts or to revisit the episode, she gives my hand a squeeze or stands up on her toes to kiss my cheek. "Forget about it, Gary," she keeps saying.

When we get to her door, I stop, remembering the last fight we had and the doubts her parents have about me. That, combined with the humiliation my father just caused me, makes me suddenly want to give up.

"I think I should get back, Lauryn," I say. "I know my dad will have some chores made up for me. I might as well get back and get to it."

"We still on for the movie tonight?"

"Absolutely. I'll be back around seven."

She asks me to come in for just a few minutes, but I can see that her parents' cars are in the driveway. I don't want to deal with them. Instead, I walk her up to her door and start to kiss her tenderly, right up against the house so I know her parents can't peek out and see us.

I motion toward the house and say, "You're not going to tell your mom on me for that one, are you?"

Lauryn just laughs at me. She explains that, despite everything, her parents still like me.

"Don't forget who their favorite kid is, though," she implores. "Don't cross me and you won't cross them."

I give her another peck and leave it at that. Lauryn disappears inside the house, and I start the walk back to my house, the sun wearing me down.

The day can't completely crush the hope inside me that things will be better someday. Somehow, I still believe that things can work between me and Lauryn—if I can just listen to her and take things slow. But then I think about where I'm going and that hope wavers, almost flickers out. I'd rather be going anywhere than my own home. What I really want to do is go by Wilson's for a few beers, but I know I can't do that before going out with Lauryn. Roverson's house is another option, but I already told him I'd come by tomorrow night. Besides, what I said to Lauryn is no lie: My dad *will* have something for me to do and will be in a foul mood for me to do it. I have to go home. All those other impulses can come as often as they want—I always have to go home. Always.

Chapter 10

Without Wilson at Roverson's I feel exposed, powerless. The place is much cleaner than the first night we were here. That's due in part to the efforts Wilson and I have given in exchange for use of the car, but it's also, I think, due to a change in Roverson himself. Every time I see him he seems a bit more in the flow of life, like breaking out of his solitude has started the world turning for him again.

Tonight he seems lively, or at least as lively as I've seen him since he left school. When I knocked he was at the door almost immediately, like he'd been waiting for this all day. Now, sitting across the coffee table from me, he turns the subject to Lindy—addressing the topic straight on instead of hinting around its edges.

"You know, I never really told anyone my side of the story," he says.

"I noticed that," I say, remembering how disappointed I was in his neglect of details. "Why not?"

He scoots his chair up an inch and leans forward, his eyes bright. All that fatigue and sorrow that seemed to cloak him is nowhere to be found now.

"Nobody seemed to want to hear my side, Gary. As soon as

Lindy told her parents that we'd been seeing each other, it was all over. Everyone made their minds up about me right away."

Seeing? I want to say that's not the word I'd use, but only Wilson has the nerve to just throw things out like that. I figure my best bet is to just have a casual conversation about it, not to push him.

"Well, I'm listening," I say.

"Gary, it's important to me that you understand this. What I had with Lindy was more than people made it out to be. I wasn't just using her. We had a real relationship."

His tone has turned serious, almost severe, and if he were someone my age I'd think he was putting me on. As it is, it makes me almost uncomfortable. Something in my face must let him onto this, because Roverson says it looks like I don't believe him.

He starts to pace back and forth in the room, and I imagine this is how he must have been when he was teaching in class. "This might be hard to accept, Gary, but we really were a couple. Every bit as much as you and Lauryn."

He looks at me, gauging my reaction. I never thought to equate my situation with his, but somehow it makes sense — there's at least a spark of recognition in me.

"But I bet not everybody accepts you and Lauryn. Am I right?"

Again I tell him he's right. He doesn't say it, but I can tell he's talking about the fact that I'm white and Lauryn isn't. There's a look people get when they refer to that without being obvious about it, a quick glance downward of their eyes like they're trying to get away with a lie.

"Right," he continues. "But those people are being so short-

108

sighted. They're trying to squeeze the two of you into their narrow-minded view, and it just can't work that way. But you and Lauryn stay together anyway, right? In spite of all that?"

He stops pacing and looks at me earnestly again, his eyes wanting, needing an answer.

"Of course," I say.

"Because?"

He keeps that same look fixed on me, expecting me to give him another answer. Problem is, I don't know what he means this time, and we endure a strange silence, me sitting there and Roverson leaning toward me in expectation.

"Because you *love* her," he finally says, raising both hands in the air.

Love. It's not a word I toss around, and it's not a word I hear often. It sure isn't a topic that comes up often in my house. I've thought about it in regard to Lauryn, but I've never said it to her—it's not so much that I don't want to say it, but I'm afraid of her reaction. I'm afraid she wouldn't say it back.

Again, when my response to Roverson is only silence, he decides to continue talking, shouldering the subject forward.

"Gary," he says. "You *do* love her, don't you?"

I manage to say, "That's a serious word, Mr. Roverson."

"Serious? I suppose, Gary. But it's also the best thing there is. You do believe in love, don't you?"

"Believe in it? Yeah, I guess."

"Gary, you *have* to believe in that much. It's the only thing that lifts us beyond ourselves. That connection with another person is what makes everything worthwhile. I mean, don't you ever feel alone in this town, like nobody understands you?"

I'm stunned by what Roverson is saying. It's like he can see

109

inside me and is turning my thoughts into words. I always feel misunderstood in this town.

"Gary, the one thing that can save you from that is love. That's what you should be striving for with Lauryn, and that's what I had with Lindy."

At this I start to balk, but Roverson raises his hand and swears it's true. He is adamant that he and Lindy had a mutual love. He tells me how it wasn't just sex, that they would spend hours together after school, sometimes riding into Indianapolis for dinner and a play, where they could be away from the shackles of town, be themselves freely. A sense of reverie comes over Roverson as he recalls this. For a moment, he seems to forget that I'm even in the room, his eyes turned away like they're focused on some distant point. He's so clearly wrapped up in Lindy it's hard not to believe what he's saying.

"I had no idea that's how it was," I say.

"Nobody did," Roverson says. "Nobody understood except the two of us."

He looks absolutely distraught when he says this, and I feel horrible for him. I imagine that if I were deprived of Lauryn I would feel the same. I feel bad enough when she pulls away from me because of something I've done, but it would be worse if forces beyond our control separated us, like what happened with Roverson and Lindy.

Of course, I can't forget Lauryn's reaction yesterday to the very mention of Roverson's name and her take on him. It seems unfair, though, that everyone has rushed to judgment without hearing his version of what happened. And, surely, if they were in love with each other, it couldn't have been that awful.

I ponder this, turning it over in my head. The problem is, I can't think straight with Roverson sitting right across from me. I wish I had more time to explore this, or had Wilson here to navigate for me.

Finally, I locate the question that's been bothering me—I ask Roverson why Lindy left so easily if she was in love with him.

"She wanted to stay," he fires back, animated again. "She told me. She wanted so badly to keep seeing me, but she couldn't fight her parents. Do you know how that is, to have your parents control you unfairly?"

"Oh, hell, yes!" I exclaim. I don't even realize I'm cursing in front of him until it's out there, I'm so eager in my response. Roverson doesn't seem to mind, though.

"Then you understand. You understand that, despite what others think, Lindy and I should be together."

I'm not absolutely sure I *do* understand, but with him looking at me so intently I nod my head in agreement. I've seen movies where a salesman just keeps pressing someone until they wilt and agree to the terms, sign the contract. This is almost how it feels with Roverson—his determination is enough for both of us.

Roverson excuses himself and goes into the kitchen. I can hear him humming in there over the running water, his tune jangling out happily. I look around the house, getting up to study pictures Roverson has displayed. On previous trips, the place has been such a mess it's been hard to notice anything like pictures. But now, I see various snapshots of Roverson. He's almost always by himself in the pictures—alone at the edge of the Grand Canyon, alone at the base of a ski lift, alone at the beach. I suppose there could always be a companion behind the camera, but it still strikes me as odd that he would never have somebody pose with him. There is one picture, though, that features a couple. It's a recent one, Roverson laughing into the camera. He has his arm around Lindy, whose eyes are cast up at him through the bangs of her blond hair. In the background, I can see the Soldiers and Sailors Monument, the center of Indianapolis, done up in Christmas lights.

With Lindy's eyes not toward the camera, it's hard to read her expression. Roverson, though, looks clearly delighted, happier than I have ever seen him. I suppose what he's saying is true: He really does love her.

Until I hear the sound of Roverson settling back into his chair, I don't even realize he's reentered the room. Embarrassed for prying, I quickly turn from the picture and sit back down across from him.

"That picture," he says. "That was from last December. We went into Indianapolis and took a carriage ride through the city. That's when things were at their best."

"I know how that goes," I say. "When things get rocky between me and Lauryn, I always think about those times that were great. That keeps me going."

"You have to keep believing," he says, almost more to himself than to me.

"Do you ever talk to Lindy anymore?" I ask.

He shakes his head forlornly.

"No. But, Gary, that's what I wanted to talk to you about. That's why I need to be able to trust you."

"You can trust me," I say. I'm not sure if I can live up to his expectations, but I like saying that, trying it on to see how it fits. "How can I help?"

"I want you to help me get Lindy back again," he says.

My insides run cold when he says this, and I feel the hairs on my arms and neck stand up. Searching for words, my mouth goes dry. Before I can say anything, though, Roverson persists.

"Will you help me, Gary? If you do, I can help you. I know things aren't easy at your age, and I can see sometimes that you're troubled. I can help you with anything. With friends. With Lauryn."

I must show him something when he mentions helping me with Lauryn, because he stops and raises his eyebrows at me. Then he starts going again.

"Lauryn? You need more help with Lauryn. My advice is working so far? You help me with my love, and I will help you with yours. Fair, right? Will you help, Gary? Gary, I need to trust you here."

"Yes," I say. Just like when we were first stealing the Lincoln, I imagine all the faces of my world looking on in judgment of my decision: my parents, the Lydles, random townspeople, Lauryn, her parents. All of them would disapprove. And even Wilson. Somehow I imagine his face contorted in a display of skepticism over my choice. He has his doubts about Roverson, though not the same kind everyone else does. He just finds Roverson odd and is slowly growing bored by our arrangement.

In spite of all that, though, I feel drawn to Roverson. It's the way he can articulate the things I feel. The way he puts trust in me. The way he thinks I'm capable of doing something more than the routine.

"Good, Gary. I'm glad you feel that way. And I know I can count on you. Let me give this some thought, though—about how to get in touch with Lindy. But you, Gary, I'll help you in any way I can."

I thank him, but I can't think of anything that needs to be addressed immediately. Roverson pries a bit, though, asks about how things are going with Lauryn. I look down at my fingers, pick at my nails nervously, and tell him things are fine. He keeps pressing, though, like he can see right through me.

As I talk to him about Lauryn, I find that I can't look up. If I keep my head down, look at the veins in my hands, the small muscles in my fingers, I can speak honestly. I get the sense that if I look up, though, I'll lose my will and just start talking in generalizations, saying things are okay. As it is, I am pretty frank with Roverson. I tell him about how I sometimes force things with Lauryn, how I want more than she's willing to give sexually, how it drives her away. I even tell him about the most recent fight with my dad, how he embarrassed me in front of her. I stop short, of course, of telling Roverson what Lauryn thinks of him. I'm not sure how I'm going to balance that out—trying to be good to both Lauryn and Roverson without letting either of them know the whole truth.

When I finish, I look up. I put my hands back flat on my thighs, and I can feel the full weight of them on my legs, like there's more to them every day. I'm hot and drained and have a light coat of sweat on me.

Roverson looks serene now, all the excitement that danced in his eyes when he spoke of Lindy now gone. When he speaks, his voice comes out smooth and soothing. No more lecture tone now. It sounds now more like a bow pulled across an upright bass—steady, untroubled, and low.

"You're a good young man, Gary. Don't you forget that. You're good enough to help me. You just take things slow with Lauryn. Remember, when you get that feeling you described,

114

like you're racing, just take deep breaths and think about how good she is to you when you make her happy. That will help slow things down. And as for that father of yours —"

He stops mid-sentence, like a song cut off in the middle.

"What?" I ask.

"Well, some of the things I think about him I'd rather not say just now."

He tosses me the keys to the Lincoln and stands.

"Tell you what, Gary. That's about enough for this evening. Why don't you go have some fun? We'll talk more soon."

With that I leave, puzzled by all the changes and challenges brought on by this evening. I have the keys in the ignition, ready to go pick up Wilson, when Roverson comes running out and stoops down to talk to me through the window. He's panting from his run, and I can see sweat forming on his upper lip. The night is like a sauna.

"Gary! I almost forgot. All that stuff we talked about in there?"

"Yeah?"

"You can't tell Wilson. This is all between you and me."

"But why? Wilson's my best friend."

"I can't trust Wilson the way I can you. And I don't mean to talk bad about him—he's your friend—but I think he just tries to use you sometimes."

This I won't take passively like his other suggestions of the night. Everyone seems down on Wilson lately, but if they could only see what he does for me, how he makes life here more exciting, they'd understand.

"Look, I won't tell Wilson. But don't say that stuff about him. He's a good friend, Mr. Roverson."

115

"Okay. Gary, I just have your best interests in mind. Just be careful around him."

He stands and takes a deep breath, and I can only see his stomach and chest, his muscles bulging out from beneath his shirt. He sighs and then says perhaps it doesn't matter anyway, since Wilson will be gone soon.

"What?" I shout. "What does that mean?"

He bends back down, his voice back to its most soothing tone.

"Oh, I'm sorry. Gary, I shouldn't have said that so callously. It's just that I know his father will most likely be moving soon, what with Dana leaving town."

"But that's not absolutely set," I stammer. "The company might still stay, right?"

He puts his hand on my shoulder, looks right in my eye.

"I hope they do, Gary. I really do, if nothing else but for you. But you should know it doesn't look good. I just want to be honest with you. It's the least I can do."

Wilson and I sit in the parking lot of the Kwik Mart, watching cars go by. Every once in a while Wilson shouts at a passing girl—*Hey, Julie, why don't you let me drive you for a while* or *Michelle, you know you want me, pull on in here*.

When Wilson calls out to them they always smile and laugh, give him a wave. Of course, if I tried that, it would come out all wrong, and they'd probably flip me off or, worse yet, ignore me.

We're perched on the hood of the Lincoln, smoking cigarettes. A half-empty bottle of peppermint schnapps is stashed in the glove compartment, the other half doing a slow burn in our bellies. What a fantastic way to escape the oppressive heat of summer—with the booze in my stomach, the rest of my body feels perfectly cool and relaxed. The only nagging discomfort is that I know the alcohol is a small breach of trust with Roverson: He'd never give us access to the car if he knew we had alcohol and has counseled us about it on several occasions. I think he knows that Wilson indulges and probably suspects the same of me, but he expects better behavior from me when I've got the keys to the Lincoln.

Wilson rolls off the hood and reaches into the car. He emerges with the bottle, waving it toward me.

"More of the good stuff?"

This is an easy way to get busted, flaunting the liquor outside, where a passing cop might see it. Never one to play it safe, though, Wilson takes a deep swig for the world to see.

"Don't you think we should be a little more discreet, Wilson?"

"Shit. Play it safe all your life, man. Have no fun. Nobody's gonna catch us. I can see any cops coming from a block away."

He shoves the bottle into my hands. I'm pretty buzzed already and want more. But I can't shed the feeling of betrayal every drink gives me.

"I really shouldn't," I say. "I have to get this back to Roverson's in one piece. I don't think he'd like me drinking while I've got his car."

"Never stopped us before, son."

I take a sip and feel the hot sweetness go down. It's good, no two ways about it. And sitting here, sharing shots with Wilson, watching the town roll by on a lazy summer night is a simple,

117

pure pleasure. I hate that things like this are becoming complicated by this sense of obligation to Roverson. Even without my newfound responsibilities with Roverson, everything with Wilson is growing complicated—from Lauryn's nagging about him to Wilson's own restlessness to the prospect of his leaving town because of his father's job at Dana.

"What is it with you and Roverson, anyway?" Wilson asks.

"What do you mean?"

"You bite on everything that guy says. And I'll tell you, doing grunt work and listening to his boring little speeches is getting pretty damn old. Not worth it just to get the keys to this piece of shit. There are easier ways to get access to wheels."

I can't have this happen. Having Wilson take sides against Roverson will make things almost impossible. I need both their forces in my life just to keep me going—Wilson to liven things up, and Roverson to calm me down and help me with Lauryn. Besides, there's a good chance I'll need Wilson to give a hand in helping Roverson get in touch with Lindy again. In spite of Roverson's confidence, I doubt I can handle that task alone.

"When I got the car from Roverson tonight, he said something about Dana and your dad's job there," I say. Inside me, the news has been welling up since Roverson said it, and I can't hold it back anymore.

"Yeah? What did that old chump say?"

"He said the company was as good as gone."

Wilson frowns. He leans up on the hood of the car and stands on the front bumper briefly, scanning the street, looking, looking. When he sits back down, he gives my shoulder a reassuring squeeze.

"Don't believe that fool. I'm not going anywhere."

He looks down the street again, and I see a flash of recognition on his face. He's found what he's looking for. He grabs the schnapps back from me and brings it to his lips, talking again right before he drinks.

"Why would Roverson say something like that? I don't think the guy likes me, to tell you the truth. I think the guy's always got something up his sleeve."

Wilson tilts the bottle back and takes another deep pull. A car goes by as he does, two girls with hair teased and cleavage busting out, the type of girls I can only dream of. They give a honk to Wilson and the driver licks her lips at him, Wilson smiling coolly back, raising the bottle to them in a sort of salute.

"Bigger and better things, Gary. Bigger and better things."

He reaches over and pulls me off the hood by my arm. Almost being dragged across the parking lot, I ask Wilson where we're going. He says the two girls in the car are named Julie and Liz, and we're supposed to meet them at the burger joint across the way.

"Who the hell are they?"

"They're the bigger and better things," he says. He explains that they're seniors at another school in the county, the younger sisters of some of his coworkers on the paint crew. As we're walking across the parking lot he keeps rattling on about how they've always got a party to go to, how hanging with them will be a great change of pace from hanging with Roverson. *That tired old fraud*, he calls him.

I yank my arm back and tell him to stop.

"Why do you always have to be chasing something new?" I yell. "And why do you have to be so hard on Roverson?"

"Because he's *boring*. Okay, Gary? The guy is boring me out

119

of my skull. I'm glad you went over there tonight without me, because I can barely stand the thought of going back into his place again."

Through the window, I can see the two girls—Julie and Liz—that Wilson and I are supposed to meet. Earrings jangling, their mouths alternately popping gum and wrapping sexily around the straws on their sodas, they give me a rush of lust. It's a million times more than the type of yearning I get when I see someone like Amber, and it's altogether different from the want I have for Lauryn. It is the same type of heat as the liquor gives me, only it hits me lower on my body.

At the same time, though, I know better than to trust that feeling. First, I want to try to follow Roverson's instructions—take things slow with Lauryn, go after something more sustaining than a quick fix. I take a deep breath and try to think of how much I feel for Lauryn, how happy she can make me, and how maybe we have something between us worthy of the word *love*.

But more than that, there's another thought that makes me mistrust my impulse to follow Wilson to meet those two girls: I know that they really just want to see him. They'll barely speak to me, and after the first few minutes it will be like I'm not even there, and then I'll hate my life just as much as I do as when my dad's pushing me around. They don't represent any opportunity for me. No, they are another exit door through which Wilson could leave me.

"Please, Wilson," I say. "Can't we save bigger and better things for another night? Can't we just hang out like normal tonight? Like we used to all the time?"

Wilson sighs. He looks tired by my hesitancy. Normally, he just keeps prodding me until I go along with him, but now he just looks like he's ready to throw in the towel. I don't know if he's giving up on his plan for the evening or if he's giving up on me.

"Where's your will to explore, Gary? Who knows, these girls could be an adventure for you."

I laugh, and for a moment I step back and see all the changes this summer is bringing, all the forces pushing and pulling on me.

"Wilson, I've got enough adventures right now. Between hanging with you, and trying to make things work with Lauryn, and trying to help Roverson, I've got plenty."

"Helping Roverson isn't an adventure anymore, Gary. He might as well be another parent. Who the hell needs that?"

Wilson motions toward the girls, his eyes wide, trying to persuade me now simply with body language.

Whether it's new people or a new town, it seems impossible to keep Wilson close to me. And when I am with him he's almost always preoccupied with an adventure elsewhere or buried beneath layers of anger. I know there's only one way to draw him back in. Problem is, it's one of the things I promised Roverson I wouldn't do. Seeing the urgency on Wilson's face, though, I get the feeling that he's only seconds from pulling further away from me. And he's never seemed like the kind of guy who slows down for anyone, who would revisit something he's already passed by. I have no choice.

"No, Wilson," I say. "You don't understand about Roverson. The thing now is that he wants me to help him get back together with Lindy."

Not missing a beat, Wilson waves at the two girls through the window and holds his index and pinkie finger to his face, a signal that he'll call them. Then he mouths the words *Gotta go*. Just as quickly as he pulled me away from the Lincoln, he starts marching back toward it. He climbs into the passenger side and I climb into the driver's.

He says simply, "Drive."

I head down the strip, the lights of all the fast-food joints and gas stations blurring together. I decide to ease the Lincoln out to the country where I'll have a little more space. I'm not that drunk, but I don't want to take any chances. Wilson doesn't say anything for a while. All the bravado he had waving that bottle around is now gone, and he seems like he's deep in thought, reserved.

I make my way out to an old country bridge, Wilson silent the whole time. In the spring, when the water gets high, kids come down here and jump off. You never know where the shallow spots are, though, and more than one kid has come away with a mangled knee or broken ankle. I've made the jump before, after Wilson talked me into it, and I came away unscathed. Adults start warning us away from this place early. Every kid in Dearborn Springs grows up with stories about poisonous snakes, kids drowning after their legs get caught under discarded tires or furniture. Of course, all the talk that's meant to scare us is exactly what makes us go. In Dearborn Springs, danger is always more appealing than the other alternatives life in this town presents.

"Shit, man," Wilson says. "Pull off here. We gotta think this one over."

We sit on the edge of the bridge, and Wilson produces a cigarette for each of us. It seems somehow cooler out here with a small wind kicking up through the leaves. Sure, the heat is still present, but everything seems calmer, in less of a frenzy.

"What are you thinking?" Wilson asks.

"About Roverson?"

"No. About politics. *Of course* about Roverson, man. What the hell else?"

We both laugh then. Perched on the bridge, I can see the moon shining off the water, which gets broken now and then by small movements at its surface: frogs, fish, insects, who knows what. When the laughter comes out, I feel like I'm laughing at the entire expanse of night.

"What do you think, Wilson?"

"No, man. He talked to you about it. This is your call. You go first, and then I'll tell you what I think."

I take another drag, trying to weigh the options. I seem to be the only one who trusts Roverson, but then again he seems to be the only one who trusts me. Fair is fair on that front. Helping Roverson will cause some deceit in regards to Lauryn, but his advice also might more than make up for it. I also figure Wilson is up for any risk there is, so it might rope him back into my life a little.

"I'm thinking, yeah, I'll help the guy out. You're up for a challenge, right?"

Wilson sighs. "This isn't much of a challenge, man. I don't like the guy. I'm telling you that now. I don't trust him. When it gets down to it, he's just another teacher trying to control us."

"Please, Wilson."

He laughs then and gives me a small shove in the back. It's enough to rock me forward, shifting my balance down toward the water. At the same time, though, he's grabbed a fistful of my shirt and pulls me back squarely on the ledge in almost the same motion.

"Don't go begging, son. Shit, I've talked you into a million things since day one. I figure I can let you talk me into this much."

He jokes that it will be good to see Lindy again, that maybe she's got something left for him, too. We laugh some more, and everything seems, for once, lined up straight in my world.

I drive Wilson home before making my way back to Roverson's to drop off his car and pick up my bike. As Wilson's climbing out of the car, I remember one last detail.

"Damn, Wilson, I almost forgot. Roverson didn't want me to tell you about him getting back with Lindy. So you can't let on like you know."

Wilson gives a big smile and rolls his eyes.

"I guess I shouldn't be surprised at that," he says. "Damn, man. What we get into."

Chapter 11

I've been taking things slow with Lauryn all week, and I can tell she's slowly starting to turn on to me. I'll give Roverson credit: His advice is gold. I've got Lauryn wanting me to kiss her more, and when she holds on to me, she presses her body against mine like she's afraid to let go. I still don't know if this is love, but I'm starting to believe.

The closer she gets to me, though, the more I want sex. But instead of pressuring Lauryn, each time I get that urge I think about what Roverson told me: that my pressure makes Lauryn feel the same way my father's intimidation makes me feel — like I don't matter. That thought usually stops me.

I've been over to Roverson's alone a few times now, and we've talked more about me than about him. It's good to have someone to talk to who is older and understands, who's already been through some of the things I'm talking about. Eventually, we always talk about Lindy, but Roverson says he doesn't want to rush into anything. *If I'm telling you to be patient*, he'll say, *then I should lead by example*.

What we have done so far is this: With Wilson's help, I got the name of the aunt Lindy's staying with up in Hammond. A little research by Roverson tracked down that aunt's phone number and address, and when Roverson says the time is right, he'll call her and try to set up a meeting between them.

In the meantime, I've been dividing my time between work, Wilson, and Lauryn—Lauryn getting a bigger share all the time.

Right now, she's got me trading lines to a play. It's silly, but she seems to like it.

"You're bored, aren't you?" she says.

"No," I say. "Maybe plays just aren't my thing. I mean, I've never really acted before."

She pushes me down on her bed and stands in front of me. Her parents are gone, and my mind is filling with all kinds of notions, but I don't let my thoughts take over my body.

"Crazy boy. This is the only way to read a play. It's fun. Come on, try again."

"Well, maybe those scenes where the characters kiss. Maybe those are fun."

I give her a little grin just so she knows I'm teasing. She smiles right back, a little glimmer in her eyes. Those eyes, when they're focused on mine like they are now, are enough to make me jump out of my skin.

"Hmmmm. All right, Mr. Smooth," she says. "You think you can handle one of those parts?"

"I know I can," I say.

We skip forward to one of those scenes, and when the time is right, I stand up and give her a kiss on the lips. I keep it simple, just a peck.

I sit back down on the bed, and she smirks at me. She reaches out and puts her hand in my hair.

"Gary. What kind of kiss was that? You see right here where

it says 'They kiss passionately'? That calls for a little more, Mr. 'I-Know-I-Can.' These characters have been in love for years, and you're kissing me like my dad's in the room."

I feel my cheeks go hot, and all I want to do is grab her and bring her down onto the bed. Just go crazy, that's what I want to do. Instead I take a deep breath again.

"Well, your dad could be home any second."

She shakes her head, gives me a sexy, elongated *uh-uh*. She puts her hand on the back of my neck now and says, "I think you should run that scene again."

I stand up and we say the lines again. This time when I kiss her I pull her body into me, planting one firmly on her lips. Lauryn responds in kind and pulls my hands around her. My fingers explore her stomach, her waist, her thighs. She gives a soft little moan into my ear.

Before I know it we're both on her bed, our hands everywhere. Beneath me, she's pulling my hips into her, and wrapping her legs behind my back. I can feel her thumbs loop under my shorts. My fingers touch her neck, her sides. Finally, I slip a hand beneath her shirt and start to ride it up along her skin. I keep moving it slowly along, trying not to rush, and then it's there, at the fabric of her bra. She gives a small gasp and then pins my hand against her ribs with her elbow.

"Not yet, Gary."

I bolt upright on the bed, short of breath. So close, so close it almost doesn't seem fair that she'd stop me now. Out of habit, though, I start spewing apologies, just an *I'm sorry* over and over and over again.

The whole time I'm nervously straightening my hair out. I don't know why—it's not like her parents are around and looking out of sorts will tip them off, not like I have anywhere else to be. I can't seem to still myself, though, part of me still rattling off apologies and part of me trying to do something with all the energy that just got snubbed again by Lauryn. I've messed it all up again.

I stop, though, when she sits up next to me and puts her hand on my thigh. She takes her other hand up to my head, her fingers warm on my face.

"Gary, why are you apologizing?"

I can't look her in the eye, I'm so ashamed. Instead I stare down at my hands, which are folded in my lap—those hands that I lost control over again.

"Because I messed everything up again. I'm sorry, Lauryn. I really am. I try to take things slow, but then I get all worked up and . . ."

"Gary," she says. "Calm down. You didn't do anything wrong."

Of all the things that could have come out of her mouth, those words are probably the last I expected.

"I didn't?"

"Baaaaby," she says. "Baby, you didn't do a thing wrong. All that stuff that happened was just fine. I like you, boy. And sometimes I want you just as much as you want me."

I lean over, kiss her lightly on the cheek. She has never said this kind of thing before. I thank her.

She smiles again, strokes the back of my neck. I want to just sink back into her hand, her arms, her body.

"But the best part," she whispers to me, "is that when I told you to stop, you did. You didn't keep pushing."

As she says this, we start leaning down onto her bed again, the kissing starting all over. I move my hands even slower this time, and again she lets me slide them under her shirt. I inch closer and closer, and when I'm almost there I get a weird sensation. It's almost like fear. I hesitate and ask Lauryn if it's okay. She pauses, then says yes.

Her chest rises to meet my fingers, and I touch her for a while. She puts her arm around my back. The strange thing is, I've wanted to do this for who knows how long, and now I'm not sure what I'm supposed to do. It's not the type of thing I can ask anybody. Am I not doing it right? That sense of fear comes rushing back in, and I stop. I pull my hand away and kiss Lauryn some more.

Maybe, I think, *if I can get her shirt off it will be easier.* So I begin to lift her shirt up along her stomach and over her chest. As I do, I duck my head to look under her shirt, and I can see the bottom of her white bra. I can't help it. I start to lean in, face first, toward those curves.

But it's not to be. At least not this day. Lauryn yanks her shirt back down to cover herself and pushes me on the forehead. Again, I worry that I've gone too far, too fast, but I can hear her laughing.

"That tickles," she says, and curls up into herself, holding her arms at her stomach.

"You're still not mad?" I ask.

She just laughs more in response. I look at the clock and realize I need to split if I'm going to make the afternoon shift at Dairy Castle on time. It's a Saturday, and things will be hopping there.

Before I go, though, I decide to press my luck just a bit. Not physically, but I figure if Lauryn's willing to get away with more in that area, she might be relaxing in others, too.

"Wilson and I are going to Indianapolis tonight," I say. "You wanna come with?"

Lauryn sits up, a serious look descending on her face.

"Who's taking you there?"

"Wilson is," I answer.

"What? He doesn't have a car. He can't drive."

"It's his uncle's car. Look, it's a little risky, but you can trust me on this one, right? He's a good driver. We'll go to Indy and hang out downtown. Wilson says he knows clubs where you don't have to be twenty-one to get in. They're underage places."

I keep my voice steady as I explain it to her. I feel like I'm completely out on a limb, but I don't want Lauryn to know that. In return, she deepens her look, and I can't tell which way she's leaning on this one.

"You still have to be eighteen to get in those places," she says.

"Wilson says you don't. And if not, then we'll just hang out at the mall. There's plenty of stuff to do there. Come on, Lauryn. It'll be all right, I promise."

It takes a few more minutes of explaining and rationalizing, but she agrees to go. I tell her that Wilson will be excited to have her come along. That much is true—Wilson might think Lauryn plays things too safe, but he likes her in his own way. He's offered before to have her come along with us when we go out, but I never thought she would until now.

I give her a kiss good-bye and ride off to work. It is a good, clean summer day. For once, the humidity is giving us a break and as I ride I feel almost right. I feel almost in control of my world, of my body, almost like a man.

*   *   *

Wilson is in good form, keeping us laughing the whole way to Indianapolis. As he drives, he's ridiculing Mr. Raymond, one of the science teachers at the high school. Mr. Raymond tips the scales somewhere over 400 pounds, and he's an easy target for the students. Wilson is impersonating him, giving us a mock lecture in Raymond's thick, curdled voice.

"Now, Gary," he says. "You're not going to, er, succeed in this science class if you can't remember the . . ."

And then he breaks in mid-sentence and rattles off a few coughs, in imitation of Mr. Raymond's smoke-damaged breathing.

". . . if you can't remember the periodic table."

Then he jiggles around in the front seat, like Mr. Raymond does behind his desk. It's a dead-on imitation, and I'm laughing so hard I have to hold back tears. Perching her head in the dip between the two front seats, Lauryn is also laughing. It surprises me to hear her in such easy spirits, considering how skeptical she was about this trip. Even when we picked her up—when I walked up to her house while Wilson idled a block away in the Lincoln—it took me a good five minutes to convince her everything would be fine.

"That's so mean," she tells Wilson.

"Then why were you laughing?"

Trying to sound serious, Lauryn explains that Mr. Raymond has a thyroid disorder and that we shouldn't be making fun of him.

"Then why were you laughing?" Wilson asks again.

"I shouldn't have been. I'm sorry." I glance back at her, and I can tell by the smirk on her face that she's putting Wilson on, that she's just trying to make him feel guilty for making fun of Mr. Raymond.

Wilson isn't that easily fooled, though. With a glance in the rearview mirror he sizes her up, and a big grin spreads across his face. This is the smile I've seen so often from him, the one full of mischief—but not the kind that leads to real trouble, there's nothing malicious in it at all.

"Maybe," he starts, his eyes still on the mirror, "you're laughing because when a guy takes up three whole seats in the auditorium, it's funny whether he's got a goddamn thyroid problem or not."

With that, Lauryn can't keep up her charade, and she bursts again into laughter. Through her gasps she keeps saying, *That is so wrong* and *You are so mean*.

The sky in front of us is a deeper shade of dusk—a deep crimson that edges into purple, blue, and black—than what we're leaving behind in Dearborn Springs, and the Lincoln is pulled toward the early evening lights of the city as if it were a magnet. Wilson lays down the pedal and we pick up speed. It's not nearly the breakneck way he drove when we outran the cops, but it's enough to make Lauryn a little nervous. She curls her arm around the right side of my seat to hold my hand. I drop my hand to my side so Wilson can't see me stroke her fingers with my thumb, a small rhythm of reassurance.

Wilson lights a cigarette and rolls down the window, the wind whipping through the car. Hot as the summer has been, the cutting wind gives a slight chill, and Lauryn squeezes my hand a bit tighter. Just with his eyes, Wilson offers me a cigarette, knowing that I won't smoke in front of Lauryn. Similarly, without words or hand gestures, I decline.

"You don't mind if *I* smoke, do you, Lauryn?" he asks.

He says it in a way to needle me, but there's still playfulness to it and it doesn't upset me. Lauryn says she doesn't object to the smoke, and with the three of us together like that—laughing, free to explore our world at the generosity of Roverson—I can't find anything objectionable in even the furthest reaches of night. Everything in front of us seems full of promise, and I silently long for us to race toward it a little faster.

When we get to Spinners, the club Wilson told us about, Lauryn lets go a large sigh of disappointment. Beside the door is a sign in bright block letters: MUST BE 18 TO ENTER.

"I knew it," she says.

I start to say that there must be other clubs we can get into and suggest again that we can go downtown to the mall. But bottom lip pouting out, eyes cast down, it's clear that Lauryn had her hopes up. I feel like I've let her down, that the magic that seemed to hover over the night is vanishing, dissolving. Our evening is unraveling, and there's a part of me that wants to give up—I've been so patient for so long, I've worked and tried to do the right thing by Lauryn, but maybe things simply are doomed not to work for me.

It's moments like this, though, when Wilson always seems to have an answer.

"Take these," he says, and hands us two small plastic cards. He starts pushing us toward the door.

I look at what he handed me and see a face smiling vacantly back. It's a driver's license for someone named Maurice Stanski, who happens to be nineteen years old but looks nothing like me. As we edge toward the entrance, I take a look at Lauryn's and discover the likeness on hers is even further off.

"What are you trying to pull, Wilson?" she asks.

"Just trust me."

"God, Wilson, the girl in this picture is so much darker than me. She's darker than my dad. There's no way I'll pass."

"Well, it's the best I could do on short notice. Your boyfriend just told me today that you were coming along."

Wilson just keeps telling us to trust him, and before I know it we're near the front of the line. Only a few people, all of them looking at least five years older than us, separate us from a muscular man perched on a stool. In spite of the hot night, he's decked out in a black leather jacket, and as each person steps up to him he shines a flashlight down on their ID and then back into their face, giving them a good, hard, threatening look.

"No way," Lauryn says. She begins to turn around in line.

"Too late," Wilson says. He grabs her and spins her back around, straight into the bouncer.

The guy examines her ID and then looks at her. He has a stud through his bottom lip, and when he speaks to say *Come here* to me and Wilson, I can see there's one through his tongue, too.

I step nervously forward, certain that we'll be busted in short order. Instead, after about ten seconds he waves us all through at once.

As we descend into the darkness of the club, I hear Wilson call back to him, "Thanks, Baxter."

"No problem, partner," the bouncer calls. "Catch you Monday, right?"

As we shuffle in, Wilson explains that Baxter is an older brother of a guy he works with on the paint crew. When Lauryn is out of earshot he adds, "Who do you think has been hooking me up with the liquor all summer?"

We're clearly the youngest people in the place, but nobody seems to mind, least of all Wilson and Lauryn. Wilson disappears to the bathroom to add some vodka to his drink, and Lauryn heads straight for the dance floor.

She's out there, bouncing up and down to a song I've never heard before. The floor is packed, but except for two or three couples everyone is just dancing like they don't know anyone else is there, like they're alone among that crowd. The place is dark, but neon illuminates the dance floor.

In the middle of a song, Lauryn motions me out to the floor, a strobe light distorting her movements. As much as I looked forward to coming here with Lauryn, I now feel paralyzed. Even though everyone in the place seems unaware of me, the thought of going out on the floor and dancing in front of them horrifies me.

When Wilson reappears from the bathroom he heads for me and offers a drink from his glass. The liquor in there might give me the shot I need to get myself out on the floor, but I don't want Lauryn to bust me. I tell Wilson I'll have to take a rain check. Shrugging his shoulders, he takes a deep drink and heads out to the dance floor.

It only takes Wilson a minute of dancing wildly, calling attention to himself, before all the bouncers and half the girls in the place are watching him. I even notice that Lauryn is watch-

135

ing him, and soon Wilson is in between two girls, grinding against each of them.

I watch one of the bouncers walk over to another and jerk his thumb in Wilson's direction. They talk to each other for a while, but I can't hear their conversation over the music. Whatever it is, it's animated and they keep glancing toward Wilson. Finally, they just shake their heads at each other and walk away.

After a while, I make my way tentatively toward the dance floor. Even though I had grand visions of this night being perfect—of me being smooth and romantic enough for Lauryn and adventurous enough for Wilson—as soon as my toes edge onto the dance floor, in the middle of all those bodies, I feel just as awkward as I do at a high school dance. At those, I just sit on the side by the bleachers and wait until Wilson gets tired of flirting with girls, and we take off to go smoke up in the bathroom. That, of course, always leaves Lauryn griping because I make a hurried excuse to leave early and never dance with her.

Swallowing my fear, I start to move to the music and I inch toward Lauryn. I'm conscious, suddenly, of every inch of my body, of my feet and knees and thighs and elbows and my impossibly big hands. It seems that in every other situation I'm not big enough—not for sports at school, not to stand up to my father. But here I'm *too* big, and I don't know how to control my body. I'm afraid I look like a fool, and I keep my head down, staring at my feet as they shuffle listlessly to the music. God, I wish I were like Wilson when it comes to things like this. I wish, sometimes, that I didn't give a damn.

It's Lauryn who encourages me this time. As the music fades, transferring from one song to another, I give her a sheepish smile, trying to look like I'm just messing around, like I

136

could *really* dance if I wanted to. She leans forward and wraps her hand around my back. She pulls me to her so our waists are pressed against each other.

"You're better than you think," she tells me. "Thanks for dancing with me."

The music rises again, and the crowd quickly picks up its rhythm, the whole place bouncing in time. Lauryn smiles at me, and I think that maybe that's all I've ever really had to do: *try*. The feeling is like holding onto a rung of a tall ladder, though, and any misstep will send me tumbling to the ground. I try to blend in with the motion of the bodies around me, try to become a seamless part of it all.

Lauryn is asleep in the backseat. We danced at the club until 10:30, stopped for some late-night eats, and now we're trying to beat it back before Lauryn breaks her midnight curfew. Lauryn's parents, in some respects, give her a lot of slack — midnight is far more lenient than my curfew. They tell her that as long as she doesn't break their rules, they'll keep them relaxed.

I used the same old excuse I've used hundreds of times — that I'm staying at Wilson's and I'll abide by his curfew. As far as my parents know, his is the same as mine. As far as anyone else knows, Wilson hasn't had a curfew in his life. My mom used to ask questions after I'd spent a night at Wilson's — *Where'd you go? What did you do? Is Wilson a good kid? Do I smell smoke on you?* After a while, she either got tired of my blunt answers or just stopped caring.

The night couldn't have gone better for me. Wilson had a

good time and didn't once seem bored or restless. Lauryn seemed to think my every move was perfect and kept giving me little kisses on the dance floor—the love that Roverson talked about isn't so foreign anymore. The two of them got along fine, even though I was constantly worried that she'd find out he'd been drinking.

The only thing now is to get Lauryn home in time, and Wilson's got the speedometer pinned at seventy-five. We'll get her home no problem. Left hand hooked over the wheel, Wilson uses his right to produce the vodka he's had stashed inside his shorts.

"Nightcap?" he asks.

"I don't think so," I say.

He puts the bottle to his lips and tilts it back.

"Wilson. Damn. You still have to get us home."

He licks his lips, getting every last drop of the vodka. He looks at me, his face turning angry. Until this moment, he'd been nothing but laughter all night, but now it's like somebody snapped their fingers and broke the spell. He looks from me to the road and then back again, and I can see those wheels turning in his head, grinding in anger.

"You know, Gary, I got one father. I don't need you parenting me, too."

"Don't, Wilson. You know I didn't mean that. Now we've had a nice night, right? Why go and ruin it?"

"Oh, I'm ruining it? What the fuck, Gary. You always want things nice and innocent. Well, face facts, kid. We're driving someone else's car, we're carrying fake IDs, and I've got alcohol on me. Shit ain't nice, okay?"

I know better than to push him on this. I just sit there with

138

my mouth shut and hope we get home okay. I look over my shoulder to check on Lauryn, but she's still completely out.

We thunder on into the darkness, the flat landscape seeming to go on forever. It's like a slate that has no end. After a few miles, Wilson laughs and lights a cigarette.

"I'm just fucking with you, man," he says. "Just playing."

I'm glad he says that, but the thing is I know he wasn't playing. He had the same look on his face he had when he beat up Merle Fuller. I don't know where it comes from, but I know I'd never be able to ask him. I just hope it passes. We're only about six miles from the Dearborn Springs exit, so maybe I've seen the last of this side of him for the night.

"Have a belt for yourself," Wilson says.

He plops the vodka down on my lap. I wrap my fingers around the neck of the bottle, feel the warm glass. Part of me really wants it, wants to share the rest of it with Wilson and just melt numbly into the night. But I know I shouldn't.

"No thanks, man." I hand it back.

"Drink, Gary."

He throws it into my lap again.

"I would but I don't want Lauryn to smell it on my breath."

I set it on the seat beside him, but he immediately tosses it back at me, using a little more force this time.

"Vodka doesn't smell, son. Nobody ever told you that?"

"Look, Wilson. Lauryn might wake up and see." Again, the bottle goes back to him.

"You're so scared. Man, she ain't gonna wake up. Just have a drink. For me?"

When he hands it back one more time, I start to unscrew the lid. But then I think about Lauryn, how she thinks Wilson makes me do things I shouldn't. And I think about Roverson, how he thinks Wilson controls me.

"No." I say it firmly and set the bottle on the dash. We're just a mile from the exit now, and I think I can hold him off for that long.

"Goddammit, man," Wilson says. This time his voice is full of anger, even more than before. "Pick that back up and have a drink."

"No."

"Do it."

There's an urgency in his voice, and I think of one last excuse.

"I promised Roverson I wouldn't drink when I had his car."

"Fuck, man! You're such a pussy. Afraid of your girlfriend. Afraid of Roverson. Afraid of everything. That loser tells you to help him get back some teenage slut and you're gonna do it, yet you won't have one drink with your best friend. And why? Because *Roverson* told you not to. Fucking Roverson!"

With that he screeches into the exit sharply, and I'm thrown toward the center of the car. The bottle slides across the dash and smacks into the windshield.

Lauryn, awake in the back, asks what's happening.

"Nothing," I say.

"Your boyfriend's a pussy, Lauryn."

"Oh, that's cute, Wilson," she says. "What are you two yelling about, Gary?"

I'm not sure what to do, so I take a deep breath and tell the truth: "Wilson wanted me to have a drink of his vodka, but I didn't want to."

We rock to a halt at the light at the base of the exit. Wilson

140

slams the car into park and turns off the ignition. He looks at me, and I know I've broken something between us.

"You coward," he says. He loops his arm around his headrest and turns to face Lauryn. "Lauryn, did you know your boyfriend is good friends with Mr. Roverson? All buddy-buddy with the town's chief pervert?"

Lauryn's jaw drops, and she grabs my arm.

"Is that true, Gary? Gary, what's going on?"

"It's a lie, Lauryn. God, don't believe him. He's just mad because I wouldn't take a drink."

Wilson starts the car again and peels out of the intersection. The whole time, Lauryn is asking him if it's a lie, but he won't answer. Instead he races through the town, tires squealing on every turn. Soon, instead of asking Wilson about Roverson, she's screaming for him to stop the car. I look over and see him grinning, amused at her cries. Through her neighborhood's narrow lanes, cars parked on both sides, Wilson floors it, getting the Lincoln up to sixty before slamming on the brakes at a stop sign.

Then, real slow and easy, he turns the corner and eases up to her driveway.

"There you are, Lauryn darling," he says. "Home just before midnight. I trust the folks won't be worried that their honor-roll daughter has been out with a delinquent like me."

She's almost in tears, but she responds to Wilson with a challenge in her voice.

"I'm not leaving this car until you tell me what you meant about Mr. Roverson."

Wilson is silent.

"Gary? What did he mean?"

I sigh. What happened? Everything had been so right, held

141

together just so. And now it crumbles into this. I should have known better than to expect things to work out for me. Still, I try to hold it together.

"Nothing, Lauryn. He was just making it up. It's a lie, right, Wilson?"

We both wait for his answer, and for the first time since I've known him I feel like Wilson might let me down at a crucial moment, that I may be crossed off from his list of friends. Preying on my nerves, he slowly picks the vodka bottle off the dash and stuffs it back in his pants. He takes his sweet time doing it, scratching his head the whole time as if he were searching for the correct answer.

"Lauryn," he says. "I made it up. It was a lie. I'm sorry."

"Okay," she says.

"I had a good night, Lauryn," he continues. "I hope this didn't ruin it."

I walk her up to her door, but all the warmth she'd shown me the entire day is gone, and all I get is a quick, passionless kiss. She doesn't even put her arms around me. It's like the mere scent of suspicion has scared her off again, like she, too, knew better than to expect something more out of the night.

Wilson and I don't speak as we drive the Lincoln back to Roverson's. As we walk to our bikes I finally break down and apologize.

"Goddammit, Gary," he says. "It's like that guy has a fucking leash on you. It's not that I'm mad that you wouldn't have a drink. I'm mad that you won't stand up for yourself."

"I'm sorry I sold you out to Lauryn," I say. "I didn't know what else to do, though, Wilson. Things have been going well between us, and I just didn't want to mess it up."

I realize I'm not even sure where I'm spending the night. I was supposed to go to Wilson's, but considering our fight that may have changed.

"Should I still come over?" I ask.

Wilson pulls the vodka out once more, a hint of his old grin returning.

"You want a nightcap?" he asks again.

"Absolutely," I say.

We stand there in the darkness, drinking. Our actions don't seem too different from how we were at the beginning of the summer. I'd like to believe that not much has changed. I know better, though.

We pedal to Wilson's house, and down the last few blocks he sprints away from me. I arrive at his door a full ten seconds after he does, and he's leaning on his bike impatiently.

"That's what I'm talking about, Gary, right there," he says. "One of these days you gotta learn to keep up with me."

Chapter 12

I know when he answers the door that Wilson's mood is just as foul as it was the other night. Shirtless, his hair uncombed, he looks like he just woke up. He doesn't say a word in greeting, just walks back into his living room, plops down on his couch.

It's been a full week since the night in Indy, and we haven't been around each other much since. I've been hesitant to call after our fight—spending my energies instead on making things right with Lauryn. After a thousand promises—lies, I suppose—that I didn't have anything to do with Roverson, she is finally starting to warm back up to me.

Inside, I see an ashtray full of half-smoked cigarettes in front of Wilson. The television is muted, but Wilson keeps flipping, anyway, not even looking at me.

"We going over to Roverson's today?" I ask.

"Why you in such a goddamn hurry?" Wilson grumbles.

I endure his silence a while longer, and then I can't help myself—I tell Wilson that, midweek, Roverson stopped into Dairy Castle to tell me he had talked to Lindy. All he needs is for me to drive up to Hammond on Tuesday night to pick her up and bring her back to Dearborn Springs to meet him. He'd go himself, he explained, but her aunt might recognize him and the whole thing would be off.

"Fine, fine, fine," Wilson says. "You can't wait a few minutes? Not like we have to go pick up Lindy right now, okay?"

I wait while Wilson shuffles off to his bedroom. The place is a mess as usual, his parents absent again. He reappears with a pint of rum and proceeds to take a few deliberate drinks.

"Roverson will smell that on you," I say. "And don't try to tell me that won't smell, I can smell it from here."

"Hey, Gary. Did I tell you I'm having a party next weekend? Maybe if you stop acting like my chaperone I'll invite you."

That news is a punch in the face. How could Wilson be planning something like that and not have told me? How could he threaten not to invite me? I know he's been making a new set of friends through his job all summer, but has he really grown that distant from me?

As much as it stings, I don't respond. Best to wait out the storm with him in this type of mood. After a while, he screws the lid back on the bottle and starts for the door. Flinging it open he looks back at me impatiently, as if to say *Are you coming or not?*

At Roverson's, Wilson looks around idly, not even paying attention to Roverson. I keep throwing him looks, trying to indicate he should pay attention, but he just mocks me. Now he's thumbing through a magazine sitting out on Roverson's coffee table.

"This all you got, man?" Wilson says. "I expected some dicier mags in your place, Roverson."

145

Roverson goes on talking to me, ignoring Wilson. I told Roverson that Lauryn is still acting cold to me after our fight—I didn't tell him what it was about, though—and he's explaining that I can't let her know that it bothers me, that I have to be strong. *Women respect strength*, he explains, *but not force*.

Wilson interjects again, his feet kicked up on the coffee table.

"Seriously, Roverson. What is this, *Atlantic Monthly*? I pegged you for a *Penthouse* man."

Again, Roverson ignores his comments and goes on talking to me. He raises his voice a bit, talking over him.

"What you can't do," he says, "is give in to every little impulse that shoots through you. Some less mature boys don't think before speaking or acting."

Wilson gives a short laugh and interjects again.

"Or maybe *Barely Legal*. I guess that would be your speed. Some hot eighteen-year-olds strutting their stuff for you. Come on, now."

That finally gets to Roverson. He stands and reaches across the coffee table, grips the magazine, and yanks it out of Wilson's hands. He slams it on the table, the magazine coming down perfectly flat to make an impressive *smack* on the glass. Roverson's flushed with anger, his cheeks and neck red. His formidable muscles are bulging through his shirt, and for a second I think he's going to reach down and break Wilson in two. Instead he speaks in a loud but steady voice.

"Mr. England. I will not have you speak to me in that manner in my house. I will not be disrespected like that. Do you understand?"

Wilson just leans back and rolls his eyes. He gives a deep sigh and looks over at me lazily.

"Gary, what the hell are we doing here? Listening to this old fool?"

Stepping around the table, Roverson nears Wilson and leans down to put his hand on his shoulder. He takes a breath as if readying to say something, but then catches a whiff of Wilson's breath.

"Have you been drinking, Wilson?"

"So what if I have?"

"You can't drink and then expect me to give you the keys to my car. Son, you shouldn't be drinking, anyway. Do you know how dangerous that is for someone of your age?"

"Spare me the lecture, Roverson," Wilson says. He tries to stand, but Roverson puts a little more weight behind his hand and holds him down.

Wilson gives a brisk chop at Roverson's hand, but he can't budge it.

"Get the fuck off me, man."

"Wilson, what are you doing to yourself? And to Gary? Don't you know he looks up to you? You should set a better example."

Wilson wriggles from beneath him and stands up, straightening his shirt. His eyes dart around the room like some cornered animal. His gaze finally settles on me.

"Let's go, man. No way am I standing for this shit. I came here to get easy access to a car for the summer, not to give some old pervert order to his life. Shit. Working around here, listening to him lecture us. It's like fucking summer school. Let's go, Gary."

I sit motionless. This is the moment I've feared for a month now—when I'd have to choose between Roverson and Wilson. I wish they could see that I need them both.

"Fine," Wilson says to me. "Stay here, chump. Bigger and

better things, man. That's what I'm after. And you obviously aren't game."

"Don't say that, Wilson."

He heads for the door, and I chase after him. Halfway down the walk I catch him, pulling on his arm. He spins, jerking his arm free from my grip, and as he does it flings up and catches me under the chin, knocking me back a few steps. I feel so helpless, and even though the contact didn't sting much, I have to fight back tears.

"You gonna cry, Gary? Figures. Give me a call when you grow up. You're fifteen, man. Time to start acting like a man, not being coddled by someone like Roverson."

Fifteen. It's not that old, I want to say. I can't be a man when I'm still just a kid. I can't even find the strength to say those words, though. Instead, I start slinking back toward Roverson, who's waiting in the doorway.

Wilson turns and gives one more parting shot.

"Have fun tracking down that slut Lindy on your own," he calls.

Roverson gives me a questioning look and puts his hands on his hips.

"Did you tell Wilson?"

"He pieced it together himself," I say.

Roverson pauses, turning this over in his head. He looks down the street at Wilson disappearing on his bike, blending into the hot haze. Roverson leans down to me, his thick, strong fingers lifting my head up.

"Did he hurt you?" he asks.

"Not really."

"You're better off without him," he says.

Before I can disagree, he puts his arm around my shoulder and leads me back into his house. Inside, we go over the plans for Tuesday night. He prints out driving directions and insists that Lindy will be expecting me. After a few times going over it, he tosses me the keys to the Lincoln and says it's mine for the weekend.

"No, thanks," I say.

"No?"

"I probably won't need it. But if I do, I'll come back by."

The truth is I have nowhere to go.

Lauryn is sitting at her kitchen table, reading. Her parents lead me in, then disappear into the living room, out of sight.

The argument with Wilson has slowly burned on me all day. It's like my life is composed of all these separate parts that refuse to stay together, and the more I try to secure them, the more they repel each other, revealing the fragility of my plan.

To make matters worse, I got home to one of my dad's fits. He was screaming, full throttle, at my mother. Apparently, she'd grown suspicious of him. *How dare you insinuate that, how dare you*, he screamed, and, *The thing is, I should be out there catting around, fucking way I get treated here I should be.* They were in the kitchen, and when I peered in he simply picked up an apple from the counter and threw it at me, catching me in the chest hard enough to leave a bruise, cursing and screaming at my mother the whole time.

Now, in front of Lauryn, I feel completely disjointed, like I'm barely myself. Knowing me well enough, Lauryn can tell something's off.

"Why don't you sit down, Gary? You're making me nervous."

I keep pacing. Just like when we were on the dance floor, I'm aware of my entire body, especially my hands. I shove them into my pockets, I put them at my sides, I clasp them behind my back—nothing seems to put me at ease.

"Can we go, Lauryn?" I ask.

"Go where?"

"Anywhere," I say. "God, anywhere but here. Let's take your dad's car and drive to Mexico. Anywhere."

"We'll go to Mexico when you let me teach you Spanish," she answers with a laugh.

I pull a chair up next to her and touch her hand. I try to do it gingerly, even though I'm racing. I've never felt this claustrophobic in my life, and I can't wait to get out of this house.

"Please, Lauryn. Let's just take a walk. Let's get out of here."

A bit puzzled by my behavior, she agrees and we head out.

We decide to take a walk through the woods that separate our neighborhoods. These trails stretch around a small pond and then meet up with the railroad tracks—the same tracks Wilson and I used to sit on, inspecting our take from the convenience store.

Lauryn and I stroll in that direction, the leaves of the sycamore and oak trees giving us shade. The path is dry and dusty, starved for rain, and with each step we hear twigs crackling and snapping beneath us. We talk idly, chat about music and television shows, until the train whistle sounds from somewhere distant. As it dies away, the rest of the woods seem silent, like all the life in them is pausing to listen for that rumble of the approaching train. A tree has fallen across the path, and we sit on it to take a rest. Soon enough, I can hear that train, the ground vibrating slightly beneath us. It thunders past and then the sound slowly fades in the other direction, but the woods seem shaken, troubled by its commotion—like these are not even the same woods. They may look the same, but there is before and after, and everything has changed ever so slightly.

Lauryn takes my hand and asks me again what's wrong.

"I got into a fight with Wilson," I say.

"What over?"

"Nothing. Stupid stuff. Nothing."

"Did he want you to drink again?"

"No, not that."

"Gary. I know Wilson. I know he smokes pot. Is that what he wants you to do, too? Is that why you got in a fight?"

"*No*," I say, growing frustrated with her questions. I just want her to treat me right, maybe kiss me, maybe let me touch her again.

She pulls her hand away from me and stands up. She looks down, the sun cutting through the woods to light up her face.

"I'm going to ask you this one more time, Gary. And I want the truth. Is there anything to what Wilson said about you and Roverson?"

"No!" I yell.

She takes a step back, throwing her hands in the air.

"Well, excuse me. You don't have to yell. It's just that you've been acting weird ever since he said that. It makes me suspicious, okay?"

I can't take this anymore. If my world is going to fall apart,

I'd rather be the one doing the destruction instead of just letting it crumble around me. I'd like to take everything and smash it up. I want to just blurt it all out to her—*Yes, Wilson wanted me to drink. And I did. And I enjoy it! And, dammit, I like Roverson, and I'm going to help get him back together with Lindy, because if I can't work things out for myself, then the least I can do is help someone else put what they love back in place. And if you loved me, if you just once could give a damn about how I feel, you'd understand that!*

I want to scream it, just let it all out.

Instead, I stand up and pull her toward me. For a few seconds I just hold her close to me, hoping all this will pass and that someday there will be a new life for me, with everything looking the same but changed in some way. God, how I want that to happen.

Then I kiss Lauryn, deep and heavy until she pulls away from me. I have my hands behind her, my fingers shoving their way down into her shorts, and I can feel the edge of her panties along my fingertips, her skin warm where it curves out just above them.

Lauryn starts to wriggle away, but I pull her back in tight. I've got her pinned to me, and I can feel her chest against mine.

"Gary," she says. "What are you doing?"

I can feel her arching her back, pulling away from me. I know I should let go of her, but I've had enough of letting go, enough of giving up.

"Please," I say.

"Please? Please what? What's wrong with you? You think because you had a fight with Wilson you can tear my clothes off?"

"No," I say. Even as I say it I'm still pulling her back toward

152

me, though. She's got her arms free of me, and as I struggle to regain control of her I tug on her shirt, pulling the tail of it out of her shorts.

With that, she gives me two rapid punches in the chest. They catch me right where my dad hit me with the apple, but they don't hurt much. Still, the impact of them is enough to make me stop.

"I'm sorry," I say.

The sound of my voice seems hollow, like it has nothing behind it, just some small whimper that the woods absorb. It's like I'm swallowed up by everything around me. I say it again, this time with a little more force.

"Save it, Gary. You're always sorry about something. I don't want apologies. I want you to treat me right."

"But I was, wasn't I? I just messed up."

"Yeah, yeah. You were, and that was really nice. But then you always get in a rush, like now. And you treat me like I'm your freaking property."

She starts toward her house, but I ask her not to go.

"Look, Gary. I'm going home. Just give me some room for a while, okay? I like you. I like it when you pay attention to me and treat me nice. I like that you finally got on a dance floor the other night, even though I knew you didn't want to. I like the way you're different from other boys in this town. I like how you want to get out—that alone makes you endearing in a town like this. But you want everything too fast. I can't do that. So just give me some room."

*   *   *

153

I arrive at Roverson's out of breath, having biked as fast as I could. Already, I'm late for dinner at home. Knowing the mood my dad was in when I left, he'll give me hell for missing dinner. He might even ground me, keep me in for the weekend—but it's not like I have anywhere worth going now that I'm on the outs with Wilson and Lauryn. By Monday, though, he'll have forgotten, and maybe that will have been enough time for Wilson and Lauryn to start to forgive me.

The only thing to do now is to head to Roverson's. I pound on his door, trying to get through this as fast as possible, like speed will help me maintain my courage. If I can get the words out fast enough, maybe I won't buckle and give in: I've got to tell Roverson I can't help him.

I feel bad doing this, but I have no choice. If Lauryn ever finds out that I'm helping him with Lindy, I'm finished for sure. And if I can wrestle my way out of this promise to Roverson, then maybe Wilson will forgive me, too.

My only hope is that Roverson will understand. After all, he's the strong one. He might be able to get Lindy back on his own.

Even as I knock, though, I have a sinking feeling. It's not just that I'm letting Roverson down—it's that his expectations made me, for the first time ever, expect a little more out of myself. I'm letting myself down, too. *No choice*, I mutter to myself, trying to solidify my resolve. *No choice, no choice, no choice*.

He opens the door and invites me in, clearly surprised by my visit. The intrusion seems upsetting to him. He's strange that way—when we first met him, his whole world seemed to lack order, but now he seems to resent any disturbance. Even when we were helping him clean the place up, he was particular about how we did it and where we put things.

"I didn't expect you until Tuesday, Gary," he says. He has the look of a kid getting busted in some delinquent activity, like he's trying to conceal a smoldering cigarette or a cheat sheet. His cheeks reveal a slight blush.

"Was I interrupting something?" I ask.

"No. No. I . . . I was just on the phone with Lindy."

I follow him into the kitchen, sit down while he pours us both sodas. His hands shake under the weight of the bottle. Or is it something else that's making him shake? He looks almost as troubled now as he did the first night we saw him, and he lets a few sighs issue while he pours. He grinds his teeth together and the veins around his temple bulge out, his eyes dark and distant again.

"What'd she say?"

"Hmm?"

"Lindy. What did she say?"

"Oh. Sorry. Everything's set to go. She's expecting you Tuesday night. You still have the directions right?"

"Yes. But . . ."

I just let the word hang out there, drenched with doubt.

"But what?" he says. His voice jumps an entire octave, like he's been jabbed with a needle. "Is there a problem, Gary?"

No choice, no choice, no choice, I keep telling myself. The light, at the day's late angle, comes cutting through his kitchen window and reflects in a bold shine off the table. The kitchen, I realize, is cleaner than I've ever seen it—the refrigerator, the sink, the counters, the linoleum all sparkling. This is a man who's put himself together and is ready to go. And here I am about to undo all his plans.

"Gary," he repeats. "What's the problem?"

"Mr. Roverson . . . it's not that I don't want to. It's that I can't. I can't go get Lindy for you."

"*What?*"

He stands up in a rush, his chair dragging across the floor. He immediately begins pacing, his chest rising with deep breaths, almost gasps.

"You can't be serious," he says. "We've set it up. We've talked about this for almost a month. We're all set to go. Don't let me down now, Gary."

"I'm sorry, Mr. Roverson. I really am. But I have no choice."

He picks up his glass, a little of the drink sloshing over its sides. He squeezes it, the muscles in his hands and forearms flexing. Either it's going to be crushed in his hand or flung across the room, I think, like an imitation of so many scenes I've witnessed at home. Instead he calms himself and sets it down. There's still color, almost rage, in his face, but it's contained now.

"What do you mean, Gary?"

"If I do this, Mr. Roverson. If I go up there and bring Lindy back to you, I'll mess everything else up. My best friend is ready to drop me forever. Who knows what my parents would say? And Lauryn won't forgive me if I do it."

"They don't have to know, Gary. This was always supposed to be between us, and it will stay that way."

"But if they do find out, I'm done for."

"They won't, Gary. And you'll be doing the right thing. How can they hold doing the right thing against you?"

"But Lauryn . . ."

"Lauryn?" he says. "Son, where would you be with that girl if not for me? You owe me. You have an obligation, Gary. The way I see it, you're right—there is no choice. You have to help me."

"Can't you go get her? It would be easier that way."

"I told you that's impossible, Gary. Her aunt might recognize me, and the whole thing would be off. It's got to be you."

I look down, my hands folded on the table in front of me. They look useless. I want to be able to help him, I really do, but the fights with Wilson, with my dad, with Lauryn, they've left me stripped of any strength. At times this summer I've seemed to gain a new power, like my body has expanded, but there is only a small ember of that left. I'm operating on lingering smoke from an extinguished fire.

"I can't," I say.

He puts his hand on my shoulder. He applies a slight pressure—firm, but I know he can squeeze a hundred times tighter.

"You can," he says. "There are times when you need to act, Gary. Now is one of those times."

He keeps repeating to me that I can, that he needs me. His voice finds a monotone and just streams along like a river, like some sequence that has no end. It keeps moving along, gaining power, gaining mass as it flows. If he says it long enough, I will believe him. Inside me, at my core, I feel a small spark catch that dying ember and its heat catches that languishing fire, small flames flickering, radiating through the rest of me. I want to act, I must act, and there is a voice telling me that now is the time. It is the only voice that has ever believed in me. And soon my voice, somewhere inside me, heated by that growing fire, is speaking with it, pushing aside the consequences that it knows are possible from all angles. All that matters is that I want to act, and that I can, and that now is the time.

It's as if I can see myself covering the hours of road to Hammond, beyond the limits of this town. Out there I'm somebody else, anybody I want to be. The end of it, the scenes that unfold once I become that person are shadowy and unknown. But I want it. I want that knowledge, that strength, that person that I can become.

I want it. I can have it.

"I will," I finally say. It is my choice.

Chapter 13

There is something maddening about the flatness of North-ern Indiana. You head up I-65 and once you get past Lafayette, civilization seems to stop. There's corn and soy-beans and intermittent farmhouses and a billboard or two, but nothing rises beyond two stories. It's like you're racing along the smooth terrain that leads up to the edge of a cliff, and any minute you'll plunge into nothingness. There are towns along the way—Remington and Percy Junction and Mount Ayr—but those places make Dearborn Springs seem like Los Angeles. It makes me think that for all the frustration I feel, there must be kids who have it even worse in those places.

On my way up, at least there is still sunlight in the long July afternoon. Then once I hit Lowell, buildings start to rise up out of the flatness, giving the landscape something vertical to look at. By then everything takes on a heavy, smudged, industrial feel, like Chicago has thrown all its refuse across the state line into Indiana.

I've been up here a few times before, summer trips when I was a kid and my dad would take us to the Indiana Dunes. Even then something always ticked him off, and we'd have to ride the whole two and a half hours back to Dearborn Springs in a cruel silence. This time, though, I head the other way on Route 20, toward the smog-choked skylines of Gary, East Chicago, and Hammond. At least I'm in a decent-sized city, I tell myself, but it seems somehow more depressing than the insignificance of Dearborn Springs.

Still, there's a dazzling freedom to being this far from home on my own, perched behind the wheel of the Lincoln like I own the road. That, mixed with the nerves I have over picking up Lindy, has me worked into a sweat even though I have the air-conditioning on high. Damn, I wish Wilson was along—he'd know just what to do to break through the tension.

The house looks innocent enough. Nicely trimmed shrubs out front. A small birdbath. The nicest lawn on its block—at least it doesn't have any debris on it. It's almost six o'clock now, and I wonder if anything is going on back in Dearborn Springs, if maybe my parents chose today to wonder what I'm up to and where I am. It will be after nine when I get Lindy back to Roverson's, and probably nine-thirty or ten by the time I make it home. If they start to wonder, I'm absolutely screwed.

I take a deep breath and knock on the door. There's no answer and I wonder if nobody's home. I'm right on time, so Lindy should be expecting me. I knock again and hear feet approaching.

The door opens and an older woman, maybe thirty-five, answers, a cigarette dangling from her mouth. This is not good. Roverson told me Lindy had picked a time when her aunt wouldn't be home. It's the right place, I know—I double-checked the address before I walked up to the door.

"Yeah," she says. Everything about her seems rough, as worn

down as the city she lives in. When she pulls the cigarette from her mouth even the skin on her hands seems coarse.

"You gonna just stand there?" she says.

"Is Lindy here?" My voice cracks as I ask it, and I feel like I'm twelve all over again. I want to run.

"Lindy!" she calls back into the house. "Some kid for you." She walks away then, not saying another word to me. As she rounds the corner into the next room I can't help but notice that, despite her abrasiveness, she has a nice body. Lauryn will look better than that when she gets old. One thing I've always been sure of is that Lauryn will keep looking better every day.

Steps come thundering down the stairs, like someone's pounding on a line of drums. Lindy appears in front of me, her blond hair pulled back in a ponytail, her mouth working over a piece of gum. She's in a ragged T-shirt and a pair of cutoff sweats.

"What?" she says.

I raise my eyebrows at her, afraid to speak. Her aunt is just around the corner and probably suspects something already.

"What does that mean?" she says.

"I'm Gary," I whisper. "You ready?"

Her face is blank. She snaps her gum. She's a number, no doubt about it. I can't help but scan her body, the way her shirt is drawn tight over her chest, coming down into a knot above her navel. The frayed threads on her sweats dangle along her tan thighs, the shorts riding high. Wilson, I remember, laid claim to those thighs. As I look at her, though, I think she might even be out of Wilson's league.

"Okay," she says. "And?"

Roverson said she might be a little hesitant, that I might have to do some convincing, but she seems completely unprepared. I remember what he said—*I'll need your strength to bring her back to me*—and I try to talk in an authoritative manner.

"Lindy. I'm here to take you back down to Dearborn Springs. I've got Roverson's car right over there." I jerk my thumb over my shoulder at the Lincoln.

"Oh, shit," Lindy says. Her jaw drops open, and I can see the gum resting on her tongue.

"What's the problem?" I say.

"Where is he?" she asks, staring at the car.

I'm completely confused now, so I decide to take a step back and motion for her to come outside. That way we can talk without worrying about her aunt. Lindy follows me out onto the lawn but never seems to take her eyes off the Lincoln.

"What is he doing here?" she says.

"Who?"

"Mr. Roverson."

"He's not here. I'm supposed to take you down to see him."

Lindy looks around and then grabs me by the arm. She's about two full inches taller than me, so she has to lean down to talk close. Her lips are so close I can feel her breath.

"What are you talking about? Tell me *now*."

Here, in a front lawn in Hammond, in a place I should know better than to be, it slowly becomes clear to me that I've been deceived.

"Roverson never talked to you, did he?" I say.

She darts her eyes about and then admits that they spoke to each other.

"Then what?" I ask. "What's the problem?"

"Well, he certainly didn't say anything about some kid named Gary coming up here in his car. What the hell? Am I supposed to just hop in and go cruising back to Dearborn Springs with you?"

The word *kid* stings. It keeps growing until I've built an anger with a good head of steam. I can't believe Roverson would do this to me. Set me up to be a fool. Use me.

I just don't understand it. Surely there has to be a mistake.

"You did say you wanted to see him, right?"

"Oh, Jesus, kid. Where is all this coming from?"

I'm tired of being played. I edge up to her so our faces are even closer. Even though she's taller, I can back her down a bit. I try to pretend that I'm my dad bullying me or my mother, try to harness that feel.

I repeat my sentence from before, but with more force—like a threat.

"You *did* say you wanted to see him."

She pauses, and then says no. "I said maybe—*maybe* – we could see each other again sometime. But under no circumstances did I say that I was ready to. God, being with him took away my freaking life! You think I'm just gonna hop back to him because of one phone call?"

"Well, I'm here now. Mr. Roverson obviously thought you were interested, or he wouldn't have sent me. Let's go."

"I can't. Not just like this. No way."

She darts her eyes around, and I can feel her considering the situation. I stay still and try to think positively. She drops her head and chews her gum. She kicks her foot into the ground, her flip-flop smacking against her heel with each kick.

"Lindy. You gotta do this. I came all this way." I hesitate over the next words, not sure whether they'll improve or hurt my chances. Then I let go with it. "He loves you."

She gives a little laugh. She looks up into the sky, and her skin looks golden. Behind her, the sun is starting to descend, turning everything from the grimy color of slate into deeper, more hopeful colors. I can see little tears form at the corners of her eyes, but I'm not sure if it's from the glare of the sun or something else.

Looking at her like that, I get a drunken mix of anger and desire. God, that face, those thighs. I want her as much as I've ever wanted Lauryn. She combines Lauryn's soft skin and curves, those fresh looks, with the promise of sex that Amber gives off. She's been had, been attained, yet is still so unattainable. Lindy seems like so many girls at once.

But I can't let go of the way she called me *kid*, the way she popped her gum and put me off and made me feel like an idiot. I want to touch her, but I'm not sure what my hands would do if I did.

"Love, Lindy," I say. "Don't you think that's worth it?"

She spins away, and then my hand does move, catching her by the elbow. I give her a firm grip, but make sure it's not too hard, not violent. But I make it clear she's not going to get away that easy. She turns back to me.

"What about my aunt?"

"Forget your aunt," I say. "You can do this. Let's hurry now."

I let go of her elbow, and I can see thin white stripes on her skin where my fingers were pressing. I soften my tone and say again, "You can do this."

She closes her eyes and takes a deep breath. When she re-opens them, I can tell something inside her has changed.

"Five minutes," she says. "Move the Lincoln. Take it down this block and then wrap around onto Plymouth Street. There'll be a big gray house with a broken-down swing set out front. I'll meet you in front of there."

With that she hurries back inside, and I can't help but think how proud Roverson will be of me.

For as much of a role as Lindy has played in my life this summer, it turns out we don't have much to talk about. I drive, even though she's the only one in the car with a valid license, and for the most part she flips through radio stations, looks out the window, and sighs.

She doesn't remember me from school at all, even when I remind her of times we'd seen each other. That hurts a little bit, but it's soothed by the fact that she barely remembers talking to Wilson. "He's the one who kept after me about how to get hold of this car," she says. "Weird kid."

Lindy does, after a while, ask how this all came about. I tell her about everything—about Wilson and me stealing Roverson's car, about Roverson coming into the Dairy Castle, the arrangement he set up with us, how Wilson helped us track her down, and how Roverson told me everything was arranged for this evening. I even tell her about Lauryn, and how she'd kill me if she ever found out about this. When I'm done unraveling the whole story for her, she just kind of laughs and goes back to the radio.

"Did he really say he loves me?" she asks.

"Yeah," I say. "All the time."

"Huh. Well, we'll see."

That's about the last thing she says until we get into town, the Lincoln taking that same weary path out those country lanes to Roverson's. At this point, I'm exhausted. I know I should be excited, returning home triumphant, like a hunter home with his catch, but the day has been so draining all I can really think of is dropping her off and then making it home to the comfort of my bed.

When I pull into Roverson's drive, Lindy plants her heels up on the dashboard and wedges her chin between her knees.

"Fuck this," she says. "I can't believe you made me do this."

"I didn't make you do anything," I say. "You wanted to come."

She shoots me a look of disbelief, her jaw hanging open. For a second I think she's going to stick her tongue out at me like a child. Her left leg bounces out a quick rhythm off the dash, shaking the car slightly as she does it. Under the moonlight, her legs seem to shine, her skin reflecting the light like water.

I make a few arguments for her to go in, but she doesn't budge. We sit there in the idling car, both of us waiting for the other to make a move. Back at her aunt's place, fueled by anger and lust, I discovered the courage to be forceful with her, but now I'm too drained to fight. Every once in a while I'll muster a *Please* and she'll shoot back a *No* or a *Why should I trust him?*

The door opens, and we see Roverson's frame amble to the car under the porch light's glow. He doesn't seem to be in a hurry, though I know him well enough to know that inside he must be churning. Lindy and I just sit there and watch him approach—she doesn't try to run or make any protests, and I just sit back and wait for Roverson's arrival, like the whole summer has been building to this moment and now all that's left is for me to simply play witness.

When he gets to the Lincoln, Roverson bends down and taps lightly on the window. Lindy rolls it down and they look at each other, neither of them saying anything.

Roverson dips his head for a few seconds and then looks back up at her, his eyes full of hope.

"Come in, Lindy."

"Why should I?" she says.

"Lindy, when we talked you said you would like to see me."

"I said *maybe*. I didn't mean now. I don't know why I let your little henchman talk me into this."

Roverson speaks again, his voice soft, almost sugary. "Maybe you were talked into it because there's a big part of you that really wanted to come."

He reaches his hand inside the car. Lindy jerks hers away from him like she's touched a hot stove. He moves slower until his hand is on top of hers, in between her knees, his fingers looking enormous next to hers.

"Lindy, just give this a chance. Come in and talk."

She looks away from him, and in her face I can see that she wants to. She wouldn't have ever gotten in the car with me if she didn't want to see him. But there is something lingering over her, some kind of doubt.

"Lindy," he says.

"Okay. Okay. I'll come in. But I need to get back to my aunt's tomorrow morning. I told her I'm spending the night at a friend's but she'll get curious if I'm not back for lunch."

"Fine, fine," he says. "Whatever you want. Just come in."

Lindy climbs out and walks around to the backseat, leans in

167

to get her bag. I take a look, her shirt hanging down, but in the night I can't see much skin.

Roverson's excitement now is evident. He can't take his eyes off Lindy even as he talks to me.

"First-rate job, son. You are certainly worthy of the faith I've put in you. From now on, Gary, I am indebted to you. You know what that means? That means anything, anything you need, Gary. You name it, I'll be there for you."

He trails off and starts helping Lindy gather her stuff. Then he slams the back door and the two of them walk toward the house. He reaches out to her hand, but she flinches again. He never looks back to me but calls out another thank-you, promises me again that he'll be there for me anytime.

I believe him when he says it, but by the time I'm on my bike riding home, doubt has set in. I can't help wondering if I've done the right thing.

I get in the door just before ten.

"It's Tuesday night, boy. What the hell you doin' out so late?" says the voice on the couch.

"Just out," I say, walking past him without looking at him.

"Where?"

"Arcade," I say.

"Bullshit. Since when do you go to the arcade?"

"Since I started going to the arcade."

By this time I've made it to the stairs, and the voice on the couch doesn't say anything more. He doesn't say another word because he doesn't really care. But after what I've done, after making that drive and coming through for Roverson, I've realized I don't care, either. I'm not going to be afraid of that man, not that sorry, drunk voice on the couch. I go up the stairs and enjoy this discovery. If nothing else, I can thank Roverson for this.

When I get to my room, I make a quick call to Wilson.

"Deed's done, man," I say.

Wilson gives a whistle into the phone. "Well, at least you got balls, I guess. For better or worse, at least you got balls."

He still sounds disappointed in me, but I know he didn't think I could go through it without him. I give him the quick rundown of how I pulled it off, and he concedes that he's impressed by my exploits.

"Lindy ask about me?" he says. I lie to him and say she did. "Thought so," he says.

"So, Wilson," I say. "You still having that party Saturday?"

"Damn straight, son."

I wait for him to invite me, but he doesn't do it. There's no choice but to ask.

"Should I come?"

"Well, I still think you're a dumb ass for wanting to hang out with Roverson. But, yeah, I'm not one to hold a grudge. Tell you what, son. Why don't you come by a little earlier on Saturday and we'll have ourselves a pre-party to put it all behind us."

"Sounds great," I say.

"And bring Lauryn that night," he says.

I don't know if she'll be willing to do that, but I tell him I'll try.

We hang up and my fingers pound Lauryn's number into

the phone. She picks up and for a while she's still cold to me. After a few rounds of apologies and admitting that I'm an idiot, she begins to let go.

"Look," I say. "I'll make it up to you."

"How?"

"Saturday. We'll go to the park after I get off work."

"Good start," she says.

"And then we'll go to Wilson's party," I say.

There's a silence on the other end.

"I'll think about it," she says.

That's good enough for now, we decide, and agree to meet at one on Saturday.

I crawl into bed, thinking back on the events of the day, the changes they're sure to bring. Tomorrow is a day off, no Dairy Castle, no Wilson, no Lauryn, no Roverson. Nothing but sleeping in and watching TV. I can't wait for that—a day in which nothing will happen.

Chapter 14

At first I don't know what's going on. My sleep was dense, thorough. Now I'm being shaken. I open my eyes to focus slowly on my mother's pained face, her lips trembling.

"Wake up, Gary. Wake up," she is saying.

I sit up in bed, in a foul mood from being robbed of sleep. I look at the clock and see it's nine-thirty. Not too early, but I had plans of sleeping until noon.

"What did you do?" she asks.

Downstairs, I can hear my dad bellowing, "Get his *ass* down here."

I make it over to my dresser and throw some shorts on, bothered that my mom barged in like that. Can't any space just be mine? Even in sleep?

I hear my dad yell again, and I start to head down. My mother beats me to the door, though, and closes it behind her.

"Is it true, Gary?" she says. "First just tell me if it's true."

I'm still in a bit of a daze from my sleep, and I have no idea what she's talking about. Whatever it is, it's raised a serious distress in her if she's willing to put off my dad's orders. I can even detect anger in her eyes—usually her looks, even when she's telling me to do something, hold more fear and pleading than they do anger.

"Is it?" she demands again.

"What? I can't tell you if I don't know what you're talking about."

"You know," she says.

"Damn, Mom. I don't."

She puts her hands on her hips. She's no taller than I am, but I get the sense now that she could knock me over if she wanted to. "That girl," she says. "Did you make that girl go back to that—that Mr. Roverson?"

She might as well have just punched me in the jaw. What the hell? How does she know? Whatever happened while I was sleeping couldn't have been good, though.

"I didn't make anyone do anything," I say. My voice doesn't even sound like mine. It sounds like it's coming from somewhere else, like it's being played back on a tape recorder.

"Gary. Don't you lie to me. This is serious. Her father just called, and she said it was you. She said you drove up to her aunt's house and brought her to him. Now. Did you?"

I concentrate on my hands. Looking at them, I realize for the first time just how much they're capable of. I decide to repeat my first answer. It's true—I *didn't* make anyone do anything. At least I want to believe that's true.

My mom puts her hand under my chin and lifts my face to look at her. On my skin, her fingers feel cold and wet. She looks right at me, her eyes moist. Dammit. As much as I resent her weakness, I can't lie to those eyes when she's like this.

"Yes," I say.

She stands up, her head down in the flat of her hand. She looks like she's mourning and, indeed, I hear a small sob escape her.

"But I didn't *make* her," I say. "She wanted to. Mom, you have to believe me. They were in love with each other. They wanted to be together."

"Love?" she says. She turns around and her cheeks are pale, her eyes bloodshot. "What do you think you know about love?"

I start to respond, but I realize I have no answer. I could tell her about Lauryn, but what am I supposed to say? I've messed everything up on that end, too. But isn't it true? Didn't Roverson say he loved her? Could the look in his eyes have been anything else? And didn't I feel the same things for Lauryn? These thoughts ricochet in my mind, while my mom keeps at me, her voice rising.

"If that's love, Gary, then I don't know what. Ha. Love. Between that grown man and a little girl. God, she's just a girl. And if that's love. If that's love, Gary, then why did her mom call us this morning? Why is that little girl sitting at her parents', sobbing?"

I can barely breathe. I still don't know what happened. I'm not sure if I want to know any more, though. I can't decide if the not knowing is worse than the knowing. In the end, though, I have to ask. I guess it's the only real option there is.

"Mom, what happened? What did he do to her?"

"He wanted her to . . . you know. God, if you're involved with this, you know what he wanted her to do. Well, she wouldn't. But he tried to make her stay. He tried to make her."

I want to believe better of Roverson, but I can only think the worst. The way my mom's talking, the way she's hesitating over every word—he must have done it. He must have raped her. Just like Lauryn said it was the first time.

"He raped her, didn't he?" I say.

"No," she says. I feel a wave of relief wash over me. Maybe Roverson didn't do anything after all. Maybe it's just the same way it was before.

"But who knows what he would have done?" my mom says. "She ran away and called her parents. Oh, Gary. It's going to be all over the news again. He's already saying that he didn't do anything wrong. That man. That *man*."

I can hear my father again, slamming the refrigerator door. I know I'll have to go down and face him. I can't stay up here behind this door forever, even though I'd like to.

My mom keeps talking. "They said your name wouldn't get in the paper. You're too young. They'll protect you. But her parents called us to let us know that you were in on it. They'll want to talk to you eventually, of course."

Cracks sound on the first few stairs, my dad's feet slamming down on them, shaking the foundation of the house.

"Gary. Now. Get down here now."

I start trudging toward the door, grimly accepting the fate waiting on the other side. As I pass my mother, she reaches a feeble hand to me and brushes my shoulder, but there is no warmth in her touch. She sniffles as she does it. She's like a ghost—you can almost see right through her, as if she wasn't even there.

There is no getting past my father, though, who's standing at the middle of the stairs. Last night, when I was too tired to care, I could ignore him. But now I know better. As much as I try to ignore him, it seems like he'll always be standing in my line of vision, fuming with anger.

"Get your ass down to the car. You like taking rides? We'll take one, boy. I swear, we're taking a goddamn ride."

I want to just run down the stairs and shove him, send him tumbling backward. But I don't. I don't do or say anything. He grabs the collar of my shirt and bunches it into his fist. He doesn't even give me a chance to brush my teeth.

I don't dare say a word in the car. I keep wondering what Wilson will think when he finds out—if he'll still think I'm brave for doing it. And I wonder what Lauryn will think. Or if she'll even find out. If they do protect my name, there's a chance she'll never know. But I can see through my own lie—this town's always been too small to keep a secret. By this time next week everyone in town will know. When the name Gary Keeling comes up, this is what will come to mind.

I assume we're going to Lindy's, so I can get it from her parents. That's fine with me. I'd just as soon get that one out of the way—I'll be paying for this one with my parents for weeks, months, maybe forever.

Then my dad turns off and heads out of town. Soon enough we're on country lanes, my dad accelerating over the gravel. With the window rolled down, and his arm slung down the side of the car, he almost has the look of Wilson behind the wheel. That's when I realize it—he's taking me out to Roverson's.

Sharp, angry breaths are the only sounds that have escaped from my dad the whole way. Now, as we near Roverson's, he speaks. "Start talking, boy."

"What am I supposed to say, Dad?"

"I want the whole fucking story."

175

"You already got it. I went up to Hammond to bring Lindy back down here last night."

He clicks his tongue at that. Nods his head. Then he slams the brakes on and we go skidding across the gravel. I feel the handle of the door dig into my ribs as we spin around. A plume of dust billows over us as we grind to a halt, and I feel sick to my stomach.

My father slams his fist down on the steering wheel, then reaches over and grabs me by the throat. He presses my head backward into the seat. He's not choking, not squeezing, but he's not letting go, either.

"Talk, boy. Tell me the whole story. He put you up to it, didn't he? I swear, Gary. You better start telling me the whole thing, or I fucking swear."

He doesn't say anything after that. I just feel his hot breath coming down on my neck as I start talking. His hand's so tight on my throat that I have trouble breathing, and I'm scared. He could kill me if he wanted to, and I want so badly to end him. Instead I give him what he wants. I don't tell him that Wilson and I were stealing the car, I jump right to the day Roverson came into Dairy Castle, wink and all. I don't have the courage to tell it any other way. Instead I just want to be away from it, I want this all to be something that happened to some other kid. Some kid I don't even know, in another town. If I tell it this way, where I have no control of anything, I can almost believe it.

"It was all him," I say. "All Roverson." And then I do something that I haven't done in front of my father since I was a little kid. I cry. The tears come rushing out, streams like an endless length of rope. I heave and pitch, and through my tears,

176

I can see the world start to move again as my dad starts driving—the trees going past, the silos in the distance, the field of soybeans Wilson and I used to sneak through, the big black Lincoln sitting along the side of the road like a hearse.

"Oh, toughen up, you pussy," my dad says. "This won't take long. I can guarantee you that."

When Roverson answers the door, my dad doesn't say anything to him. My dad doesn't ask to come inside, he doesn't ask what happened last night with Lindy, how I was persuaded into helping, or what Roverson has to say about it all.

He just puts his hand square in Roverson's chest and pushes him back inside. I try to tug on my dad's arm, then on the back of his shirt, but it's useless. It's like trying to restrain a rhino with a leash. I have no choice but to follow in and watch: Even though part of me wants to cover my eyes, there's a gnawing hunger to see this confrontation.

Roverson stumbles backward until he reaches the base of the stairs, where he catches himself on the banister. He's taller, more athletic than my dad, but he doesn't have that deep-seated rage to feed him.

"Mr. Keeling," he says.

"Don't mister me," my dad says. His hands are at his side, but he's rocking back and forth on his feet, like he might burst into action at any moment.

"Mr. Keeling," Roverson says again. He's in the same clothes as last night, and his face looks wasted and chalky. Fatigue and hurt are all over him and seem to leak out of his eyes. I've never seen a corpse, but Roverson is close enough. "Mr. Keeling, you don't under—"

The last syllable has no chance of making it out of his mouth, because my father's fist is too busy smashing into his teeth.

Roverson tumbles back, his hand slipping from the banister, his skull cracking against one of the stairs. He keeps trying to yell out a protest, but my dad never gives him a chance. There are shots to his face, his chest, his stomach, and soon the only thing emanating from Roverson is a prolonged moan punctured by higher pitches when the blows make impact.

I'm frozen, but with each punch my dad lands, I can feel something bruising, breaking, shattering inside. He might as well be hitting me.

Finally, Roverson curls his arms in front of him for protection and scrambles up the stairs, my dad pursuing him. A small cut on Roverson's forehead is leaking blood, his mouth is already swelling, and his shirt is torn at the collar. With a chance to catch his breath, though, Roverson is prepared for more, his fists up in threats of a jab at my father.

"You come within a mile of my son again and you're dead, Roverson."

"Just give me a chance to explain, Mr. Keeling. Lindy wanted to stay here, but when she called her aunt to . . ."

My father gives a scream then. "Oh, fuck, Roverson. Save it. I don't give a shit about that little tramp. Hell, do whatever you want. But you bring me into it and then I have to deal with it. Goddammit. I don't need her parents riding my ass. I don't know if they'll throw your ass in jail for fucking Lindy, but maybe they can for turning my son into a delinquent."

As my dad speaks, Roverson's hands slowly drop back to his sides. The color that had rushed to his face all drains again. Except for the marks my dad left, Roverson looks even more ashen than before.

"I didn't make him do anything," Roverson says.

My father simply spits on the floor.

"Gary, tell him," Roverson pleads.

They both look at me then, my father scowling over his shoulder. I open my mouth to speak, but nothing comes. Nothing. I've never hated my father more than I do right now, but I've never been more frightened of him, either.

"Gary," Roverson says again.

"Get to the car, boy," my father says. Slowly, I start to turn and walk back outside, but I can still hear my dad speaking to Roverson. "You're done, mister. Save your excuses for the newspapers. What you went through the first time? Shit. That's nothing compared to the hell you're in for now. Have fun."

Back in the car, my father starts to laugh in loud, sharp blasts. Like gunfire. I try not to cry. I try not to breathe. All I can think about is how I let everyone down, how my actions last night betrayed Lauryn and my nonactions this morning betrayed Roverson. I wish, really, that I could simply not be.

I look at the clock in the car and it's not even eleven. I was supposed to still be in bed.

Chapter 15

I wake up, and they're already into it. Who knows what it is this time—it can start over something as simple as a cable bill, as small as being out of orange juice.

From upstairs I can hear her say *I still think it's sad. Christ almighty*, he says. It goes on and on from there.

It's hot already, muggy, so I shower right away. I have to make my shift at the Dairy Castle, then I'm meeting Lauryn in the park, followed by Wilson's party tonight. My parents grounded me for an "indefinite period of time," but after two days they've already lost interest. Besides, I told them I'm working a double at Dairy Castle and that tonight I've arranged to talk to Lindy's parents. I figure by the time I'm supposed to be home, my dad will be too drunk to care if I'm later than expected. Just another Saturday in our house.

I come downstairs and hear him say, "The guy's a coward. What else would you expect?"

"That's enough," my mother tells him when she sees me.

I walk to the fridge and grab a soda.

"Don't let that be the first thing on your stomach. Do you want eggs? There's some sausage left."

"Let the boy eat what he wants. Christ, he's old enough to get in man-size trouble. He's old enough to decide what to eat."

"Eggs are fine," I say, and open my soda. He lights a cigarette and watches me.

She pulls eggs from the fridge and cracks them, starts scrambling them with cheese, onions, peppers. She gets more salt from the cupboard. They're on the same side of the kitchen island—her cooking, him smoking by the window, a plate of half-eaten sausage below him. It's crowded and when she bends down to adjust the burner she bumps him. He grunts and slides his plate down the counter toward the coffeemaker. He decides to refill his mug, stooping above it as he does. He stands and cracks his head on the corner of the cupboard door.

"Ouch. Fucking shit, ouch!"

"What?" she says, startled.

He slams his mug down and looks at her. Coffee splashes on the counter, the floor, his pants.

"How many times have I told you to keep these fucking cupboard doors shut?"

"Nice language," she says, and tilts her head toward me.

"*Nice language*," he says, mocking her. "Think the boy's never heard that word before?" He has the cruel, sneering tone of a juvenile. They glare at each other as he rubs his skull. She starts toward him and he looks away, peering at the window, the fraying blue drapes. He takes a drag on his cigarette.

"Fix the boy his eggs," he says, and motions to the stove with his thumb. He blows smoke to the window. When she turns back to the stove, he swivels his head to his shoulder so he can watch her. He's ratcheted up his mood since Wednesday's news

.

181

about Roverson and Lindy, like the whole affair is a burden on him. I can see now he'll use it as an excuse to bully us every waking second. I can almost accept him doing it to me—I'm the one who got involved—but he treats my mother like everything is her fault, too.

She brings the eggs to me with a glass of milk.

"Thanks," I say.

"You're welcome," she says, and brings the salt and pepper. My mom isn't going to forgive me anytime soon, either. But with her it's more disappointment than anger, and I can tell she just wishes the whole thing would disappear.

She lights a cigarette and walks into the dining room, lifting the newspaper from the counter on her way. He watches her go in and sit.

"Where you off to today?" he says.

"I told you. I've got a double at Dairy Castle," I say. I shake salt on my eggs.

He goes to the stove and scrapes more sausage onto his plate. He looks into the dining room deliberately. He leans against the counter in the middle of the kitchen and clears his throat. He walks to the refrigerator and takes out a beer, opens it. He walks back and leans on the counter.

"You come straight home after that, boy," he says.

"Sure," I say. I tell him that I might need to stop by Lauryn's to pick up a CD I left there, just a little lie to try and carve out some more time.

"Hell, no. Guess you won't be seeing much of the little negrita for a while, huh?"

I drop my fork on my plate. He looks at me, waits for me to say something. His look, his waiting, make me hate him more.

I want to be strong enough to hurt him. I want to have the right words to explain how ignorant, how horrible he is. Anything to change that look—throw my plate at him, jump him with my knife, laugh at him, yawn, anything. He keeps staring at me and takes a drink of his beer.

"Problem with that?" he says.

I finish eating and walk back upstairs. I hear him walk into the dining room and sit down. He's not done with her. Not by a long shot.

I sit down on the bed and pick up the phone.

"Lauryn," I say when she answers.

"Hi, baby," she says. Her voice is secure and positive. After I got back with my father from Roverson's the other day, I managed to get a call in to her. She, like the rest of the town, already heard about Roverson trying to get Lindy again. The news about my involvement, however, had been withheld. Judging by her tone now, she remains suspicionless. In time, though, it will come out. I need to figure out a way to tell her myself, and soon.

"Are we still meeting at the park?" she asks.

"Yeah," I say. "I need to stop by Wilson's for a second after work." Downstairs I hear something fall, then the sound of him opening the refrigerator again.

"But you'll see Wilson tonight," she says.

"I just have to help him set up for the party. You're coming to that, right?"

"Maybe. Depends on your behavior at the park," she says.

We hang up, and I instantly get the sense I should have said more. I even get the urge to call her back and tell her I love her. Everything makes me feel desperate. There's nothing to do, though, but go to work. I go downstairs and walk to the door.

I can hear their argument continuing.

"Why it happened doesn't make a difference. He's gone. It doesn't matter," he says.

"Don't you see?" she says, "that's *why* it matters. That's precisely why all of it matters."

I close the door and bike to work.

I'm in no mood to deal with Frank's stupidity, so when he starts asking what all goes in the super burrito, I tell him to figure it out on his own.

I sulk to myself, dully working through orders and trying not to make eye contact with anybody. More than ever, I have the sense that the next customer is going to recognize me, strip bare any disguise I'm trying to put up and call me out.

Up front, Lydle and Marny are deep in discussion.

"If you ask me, this town should be throwing a party," he says.

"Oh, I don't know. That seems a bit harsh. But maybe we can all finally put it behind us," she says.

Though it's nothing similar in the level of volatility, the subject matter sounds the same as what my parents were talking about. As much as I want to be invisible, it snags my attention, and I can't help but ask.

"What happened?" I ask.

Marny takes off her glasses and starts wiping them on her shirt.

"That man, that, uh, Mr. Run, er, what his name?" She looks at Lydle, squinting, as if she might be able to locate the right word if she could only focus her vision.

"Roverson," Lydle says. "Sonofabitch."

I want to know and want to be protected from the truth all at the same time. The question must be written on my face, though, because Lydle keeps on.

"A reporter went to his house to track him down yesterday, but there was nobody there to find. Guy split town. Damn guy couldn't face the music a second time, I guess. Damn fool."

"No," I say. Even though Roverson set me up, the news makes me feel like a piece of me is missing, too.

"What," Lydle says. "You think it's heartbreaking? That's what some people are saying. Boo-hoo for the bastard. All these bleeding hearts saying the town shouldn't have been so hard on him. Well, ask that girl's daddy what he thinks. Only tragedy is Roverson isn't around to get what he has coming."

Lydle's tone sours me. It's not like I feel for Roverson, but for everyone in this lousy town to make up their mind about it without knowing the whole story makes me sick. Thing is, I'm next. Once it starts leaking out that I was involved, the Mr. Lydles of this place will treat me the same way. It will be a rush to judgment, and I'll never get a chance to defend myself.

I'm just repulsed by the whole thing. In fact, Roverson's solution—running—doesn't seem like a bad idea. Anywhere would be better than here. Only problem is I don't have a place to run to.

"You talk like you know everything about it," I say. The words start pouring out, like the whole summer I've been walled up behind deceit, brick by brick, and now the dam is breaking free. "What's wrong with you? With everyone? Maybe there's more to something than the general wisdom of Dearborn Springs has room for."

185

Lydle's eyes flare at me in anger. Behind him customers are starting to peer at us, curious over the noise.

"Watch your tongue, kid."

"Watch yourself," I say. I've had enough of this job, enough of Frank screwing up and Marny mispronouncing my name. Enough of Lydle's narrow-minded take on the town. In fact, if I'm doomed to be judged just like everyone else then there's no reason for me to take one more second of this place. I rip my apron off and throw it on the floor, raising my voice into a yell. I figure Lydle's embarrassed enough teenagers over the years; it's time for one to get him back. "In fact, go to hell."

"You just lost yourself a job, boy," he says. His face is bright red, his veins raised.

"Keep your fucking job," I say. I yell it over my shoulder as I head for the door, but I know I'm yelling just so my noise will drown everything else out, at least for a while. I feel a jolt of energy as I leave the kitchen behind me for good. As soon as I take a few steps in the mid-July heat that energy fades, though. There are some things I can't quit, can't change. I look around and know I'm still in the same old place.

I cross Wilson's yard and the neighbor's dog starts barking, the links of its chain pulled taut.

I've been riding around for an hour, trying to race away from the news, like if I ride fast and far enough I can undo it—all of it.

I sit outside Wilson's house before going in, trying to settle myself down. The paint on the house is peeling. A dilapidated Chevy rusts in the yard, the glass reflecting the sun. I hop on the hood and feel the metal burning me through my shorts, so I remove my shirt and sit on top of it for an extra layer of insulation.

"Wilson," I finally yell.

His head pops up from beneath the front window. He's been lying on the couch watching TV. He puts his arm out the window and waves for me to enter, so I hop from the hood and throw my shirt over my shoulder, feeling the heat from the metal trapped in its fabric. The house is in disarray, the kitchen smelling foul. Wilson walks over and slaps me on my bare back, stinging it.

"What up?" he says.

"Not a thing," I say. I decide to let the subject of Roverson and Lindy simmer. Maybe Wilson hasn't heard, or maybe if I just ignore it, it will somehow vanish. No, I know better than that, but I don't have to be ready to deal with it just yet.

Wilson's shirt is off, too. It's stifling in the house and the ceiling fan is humming, creaking in failure against the heat. Wilson's drinking a beer and offers me one.

"I'm meeting Lauryn later," I say, shaking my head no.

He lays back on the couch and I sit on the carpet. There are stains everywhere, splotches of unnamed matter dotting the floor. He picks up the remote from the coffee table, covered with empty cans and a large, dirty ashtray. Disinterested, he flips through the stations.

"You're still coming to the party, right?" he says.

"Uh-huh. Lauryn's not sure if she wants to, though."

"I like Lauryn," he says. "I mean, she holds you back sometimes, but she's not that bad. I wish she'd come."

"She will," I say. This probably isn't true, but as long as I'm avoiding the truth, I might as well do it on that front, too.

Wilson tosses me a cigarette, saying I can at least have a smoke before going to meet Lauryn. We sit there, smoking, watching videos, cartoons, a black-and-white movie.

"How's the folks?" Wilson asks.

"Fighting," I say.

After a few smokes, I borrow some deodorant and a mint from Wilson, hoping to mask the smell on me.

"Trying to get the stink off you?" Wilson says.

"Yeah."

"It's gonna take a lot more than that, don't you think?"

He's wearing a grin when he says it, and I give a little laugh, but I'm not sure what he's talking about. I shrug my shoulders and sit down next to him. He just keeps grinning at me, though, waiting for a response. After a few seconds, I shrug at him again and turn my palms upward, wanting to know what he thinks is funny.

"Yeah," he says. "You got a serious stink on you. Smells like you got a bunch of trouble stuck to you. Roverson-sized trouble."

I wince. There's no escaping it, even here.

"It's not my fault," I say. "Wilson, it isn't."

He laughs, coarse and callous.

"Don't laugh about this, Wilson," I say. I feel myself trembling, and I feel sick to my stomach.

"Oh, yeah, big boy Gary unleashed a whole lotta hell. You know, I was right about that guy," Wilson says. "When they searched his crib they found a few teen mags left over. He couldn't fit them all in the suitcase, I guess."

He laughs again, then, like it's the funniest thing in the world. I stand and cross to the other side of the room.

"That's not true," I say. "And this isn't funny, Wilson. Don't do this to me."

"I'm not doing shit to you, man. But you gotta admit it's a little funny—a grown man tucking tail and running off in the night over some girl as easy as Lindy."

He twists his face into a mockery of sadness, pretending to be Roverson, saying *Oh, Lindy* over and over.

"Don't," I say again, but I know he doesn't hear me—or if he does he isn't listening.

"Shoulda listened to me, son. Shoulda listened to me." He's stopped laughing now, but his smile is just as sickening. He bares his teeth at me in a little I-told-you-so sneer. I tell him to back off on this one, but that just incites him more. This is his triumph, I guess. When he's had enough of it, though, he just pats me on the shoulder and tells me to lighten up.

I slap his hand away. "Don't you touch me," I say.

"Ohhhh, Gary still thinks he's big. Look, man, I was just giving you a little hell. Get over it. I thought we were gonna go back to getting along just fine."

Why? Why does Wilson have to do this to me now when I need him more than ever? I want to plead with him, but I'm tired of asking. I hang my head down.

"Wilson," I say. "How can you do this? You know I didn't mean for any of this to happen."

He laughs again, louder than ever—one big, echoing *Ha*. When that sound stops, all I can hear is that ceiling fan whizzing around, racing like mad to get nowhere.

"When are you gonna wake up, Gary?" he says. "That guy used you and you still can't see it. Goddamn. Get over it. You fucked up, but so what? Or are you gonna start moping around

189

like Roverson? Man, you two deserved each other. Maybe you can still catch him if you hurry—you'd be able to recognize the car, right?"

From his voice, I can tell he's turned the corner into anger. He's got the condescending tone he gets when he's frustrated with me. He cuffs me on the back of the head, hard.

"Stop it!" I scream. "Why can't you just help me?"

"What? You gonna fight? Figured you'd just run like Roverson."

He cuffs me again. And then I can't stop myself. We go crashing back into the coffee table, the debris on it scattering onto the floor. I feel his fists clanging against the back of my skull, my head buried into his chest. I can smell his sweat, feel his hot breath in my hair. I close my eyes and just keep punching, sometimes getting air, sometimes landing on his body. I don't even know what or who I'm fighting, it's just blind motion. The whole time I keep yelling at him, the words *Just help me* issuing from me like a chorus.

He finally gains control of me and hurls me off him. I go tumbling toward the door. I stand up, out of breath and sweating. The silence now is as scary as anything else.

"Wilson," I say.

"Shut up. Get out. I guess I won't be seeing you tonight."

I leave before he can see my tears starting to build.

I put my shirt on and return to the day's steaming heat, the screen door slamming behind me. A breeze has started and I can hear the shutter bang against the house. The dog barks at me again, running up only to be jerked back with a loud clank of its chain. Part of me wishes the dog would break loose and just lay into me, let its teeth rip me to pieces.

*   *   *

When I arrive I see Lauryn sitting on a bench in front of the stream. The band, a local one, is across the stream and beyond a small gathering of people on the lawn, playing loud, sloppy jazz in the pavilion. She's wearing a white shirt spotted with prints of dandelions of varying size. It is the kind of shirt I think only she can get away with wearing. She's wearing a blue baseball cap turned backward. I lean against a tree and watch her from behind. She is small and thin, almost fragile, like something just out of the egg. She leans down and scratches her leg with her long nails, and I notice she's not wearing any socks. Her white tennis shoes shine in the sun against her small ankles. Her calf flexes as she scratches it, smooth and taut.

I walk up behind her and take off her hat, kiss her on top of the head. She looks up and I smile down at her, trying to exude a sense of calm and happiness.

"Hey," I say, still grinning.

"You're late," she says. She grabs her hat back from me and folds her arms across her chest, staring at the band.

"Sorry," I say. I sit down beside her. We sit on the bench together, listening to the band. Finally, she lets me hold her hand.

"How was Wilson's?" she asks.

"Never mind," I say. "Forget the party tonight."

"Gary," she says. "What happened?"

"Please, please, please, just let it go," I say.

"Fine," she says, but eyes me with suspicion.

She says she wants to listen to the band. I start to talk, but before I can finish the first word she interrupts me.

191

"Listen to the band, Gary," she says. "I can tell you're worked up, so just relax and listen."

I look at her, the sun a crown of light above her shining skin. God, if I could only have her maybe things would be okay. Maybe I can still hope for that. Just that.

I sit next to her and we listen some more. After a while I put my hand on her knee. There's an urge to move it farther, to slide it up her thigh. I know, though, that she's in no mood for that. And I realize that, despite my wanting more, I can be satisfied just with this—with sitting peacefully with my girlfriend, listening to the music and enjoying the day. I know I need to talk to her, though, to tell her what's happened.

"Lauryn," I say.

"Shhhh," she says, shaking her head and laughing. Her eyes are cryptic and beautiful. How could I have let her down? She's sitting there, smiling, not knowing what I've done. Still, if I can lead up to it right, I can make it make sense. She has to understand. She has to.

I take her hand in mine and put them both back on her knee. She smiles. The band finishes and we sit there holding hands as people file away, migrating to concession stands and the water slide. The air pressure is stupefying, and clouds gather in the west. A storm will be here soon. I feel like we are a part of the landscape, part of the clouds moving in and the heavy air, as if the entire crowd were struck down, we would be the same—here together as part of the world. That is what I want—the two of us and nothing else.

I can hear the wind pick up. I hear the bounce of basketballs from the courts, the lifeguards yelling out admonitions. We're quiet for a while and she lets me kiss her.

"Will we ever get out of here?" I ask.

"Dearborn Springs? I thought you were working on that."

"I could be a doctor," I say.

"You won't be a doctor hanging around Wilson," she says.

"Stop it," I say.

"What am I gonna do?"

"Be a model."

"You can do better than that," she says. "I want to do something with my mind." She elbows me when she says *mind*.

"Okay," I say. "You write. Best-sellers about some lousy Indiana town. Everyone will think your books are quaint and kind of sad, but we'll know they're uplifting because we don't live in that town anymore."

"Gone from Dearborn Springs?"

"Straight out."

"Where do we live? What about Boston, or New York?"

"Or west. Southwest. Phoenix or Denver."

"Denver sure beats Dearborn Springs," she says. She laughs.

"We'll get straight out," I say.

We stare down at the stream, see the reflections of the clouds moving in it. It's a wide, tranquil stream that leads to the Wabash River. That river turns and goes south toward the border where it meets the Ohio, and then just keeps going. I have a horrible sense that all our words will amount to nothing. Nothing will ever change. I'll never get out of here, or be a doctor. We'll just go on like the water, meandering into the unknown, but never changing. The clouds will keep moving, my parents will keep fighting, I'll always wind up wanting more from Lauryn. The only thing that has to change is that I can't keep the truth from her any longer.

"I have to tell you something." I say. "It's big."

"Go ahead, Gary. I'm all ears, crazy boy." She smiles when she says this, and the smile makes me hurt more than ever.

"It's about Roverson."

"Oh, him." Her smile vanishes. "I can't believe what he did. How horrible."

I want to undo it all. But more than anything, I don't want to do the one thing I have to—tell Lauryn that it wasn't all Roverson's doing.

"It wasn't his fault," I say.

"What? How can you say that? What's wrong with you?"

"Lindy wanted to come down here, Lauryn."

That sentence lights a fire inside her.

"How do you know that, Gary? How?"

Hell with it. I might as well get it over with.

"I know because I'm the one who brought her here. She wanted to be with him."

Lauryn doesn't say anything in response. She just starts slapping at me, catching my ears, my neck, my shoulders. I try to grab her and pull her to me, but her arms are moving too fast.

"Why? Gary, why would you do that?"

"I did it because I love you." I know it must make no sense to her, but I can't think of anything else to say.

A horrible, pained look comes across her eyes, like something inside her has split apart. Her brow wrinkles up into three deep lines, and then she gazes past me, back where I know those clouds are billowing big and dark.

"How can you possibly say that?" she asks. "How could you have possibly done that for me?"

She looks at me intently, waiting for an answer. I have no choice but to spill the whole thing again. This time, though, I start at the very beginning, coming clean about Wilson and me stealing Roverson's car. Lauryn doesn't say anything as I talk, but her face keeps sinking further, so after a while, I'm talking to the top of her head, her eyes at the ground. I finally get to the part about Roverson convincing me to take things slow with her, and I feel utterly exhausted and drained, like I'm bleeding instead of talking.

"You have to admit, Lauryn, that things were getting better between us," I say. "Until the last few days they were. You have to admit that much at least."

She sighs, but at least she lifts her head back up to look at me.

"That taints it all, though, Gary. That means it wasn't even you acting that way—it was somebody else. That just makes me feel sick. I feel disgusted."

"But, Lauryn."

"But what? All I wanted was a regular boyfriend, Gary. Not some huge conspiracy."

I feel like kneeling. Either that or just falling down completely, because I barely have the strength left to stand up straight.

"I just wanted to do right by you. You have to believe that. The last thing I wanted to do was hurt you. Please. If I could undo all of it, I would. God, I just wish I could start over."

I reach out for her hand, but she smacks mine away.

"You want to start over?" she says.

"Yes. More than anything."

"Fine," she says, but she folds her arms. "I'll let you start over. Square one. I won't turn my back on you now." She gives a hesitant laugh. "You're gonna need a friend more than ever when this stuff gets out."

"Thank you, Lauryn. Thank you."

I reach out to hug her, but she pushes me away.

"Whoa. None of that, though. Square one means square one. I will be your friend, but not your girlfriend. You are a completely different person to me, and as far as I know, you're not one I want to have hugging and kissing me. Starting over doesn't mean picking up where we left off. I'll be here for you, though. Deal?"

I agree, but then we don't know what to say after it's settled. I kick at the grass and mutter a few more apologies before she goes.

Chapter 16

I walk in the door and the skies are starting to spit behind me. Inside, things have slowed. They're in separate rooms, smoldering. He's drunk in the kitchen and watches me walk across to the television. I reach for it and he coughs.

"Upstairs," he says. "Use the TV upstairs. I'm going to put on some records."

I make my way to the stairs and hear him open the fridge. He starts to sing, his words warbling dangerously throughout the house. The front screen door slams, and I hear the windows shake as the winds hit them with the first heavy drops.

"Tell your mom to come down here," he says.

I get to the top of the stairs and look into their room. She's sitting upright on the bed, her back supported by pillows. The room is dark with the storm, and the TV flickers on her face—a weak, sick light. She's smoking.

"Mom," I say.

"I heard him," she says. Her eyes are red and she takes a nervous puff. "I'm not going down there."

"Mom," I say, but she won't look at me. I start to walk away.

"Gary," she says when I'm almost to my room.

I walk back to her doorway again. She waves me in and when I get next to the bed she puts her hand on the back of my head. She won't look at me, though, not directly.

"It's going to change," she says, but I just sigh. "I *mean* it. He'll learn someday that he's an asshole. Or we'll learn." She looks at the TV as she says this, and I expect her to blurt out a *Jeopardy* answer any second, because the conversation is far more trivial than anything on that show.

I just stand there. She won't even look at me when she says these words, these same, dead words. She doesn't have the courage it takes. Or the right words, either. None of it.

He puts on a record downstairs, scratched and reedy. She turns the television volume up, way up. He retaliates, raising the level of the stereo. It goes on like this as the storm kicks up outside, letting go rain and thunder.

He yells up, again. "Is she coming down, boy?"

"No. She's not feeling well."

There's a pause. Then the music clicks off.

"Then I tell you what? Why don't you bring your ass down?"

I descend the stairs, like I'm sinking into water. When I get to the bottom, he tells me from the couch that he wants to talk to me about something.

"What is it?"

"You liked that old guy Roverson, didn't you?"

His tone, amazingly, sounds almost contrite. I edge toward the couch.

"Yeah," I say. "Besides Wilson, he was just about my only friend."

"You sad he's gone?" he asks.

198

"Yes," I say. I want to reach out to somebody, even my father.

"Well, let me tell you something. My only regret is that I didn't get to chase him from town myself."

He turns and looks at me, proud of himself for the comment. His eyes droop with alcohol, but it can't hide the pleasure in them. I swallow, everything tasting acidic. My limbs are cold, like they're not even part of my body, but in my gut I feel an intense burn.

My dad's not done talking, though.

"And as far as that little punk Wilson, well, he might as well be gone, too, as far as you're concerned."

I manage to ask why through my dry, numb mouth.

"Because I say so. Either he's out of town on the rails with Dana, or we'll move so you'll go to a different high school than he does. I never liked that prick, anyway."

The burn inside me flares now. Even if Wilson threw punches at me today, none of those hurt as bad as my father's words—each one of those falling on me like an anvil. Even when I walked out of Wilson's house today, even after what he said, I never thought it would be the last time I'd see him. No. I never thought that. It just can't be.

"No!" I scream. And then I'm running, shoulder lowered, until I slam into the brutish slab of flesh that is my father.

"No," I keep screaming as we topple, both of us crashing down onto the living room floor. I start swinging at him, catching his dull eyes by surprise, and I feel the glorious impact of my fists into his face.

Punch. Punch. Punch. Punch. I try to get one in for every single word he's said, for every time he's pushed me around, for every time he's scarred my world. Saliva flies from my mouth as I scream and curse and froth. I see my hands flying in a blur, seeing for the first time how big they are, how much damage they can do.

But then I'm being lifted, my feet off the floor, one of his hands under my arm, the other with a fistful of my hair. Then there's nothing on me but air, my body sent hurtling over the coffee table, toward the entertainment center, everything whirling away from me. For a moment, I'm weightless, insignificant, free of all the horrible gravity.

And then I hit, raising a tumultuous clatter. My head connects with something sharp, and everything goes dark for a second. I can feel the blood starting to flow out of me, though.

My eyes open in time to see his fist coming down, and I feel the wild, intense pain of its momentum on my jaw. I yell, but my sound is cut off when his foot swings squarely into my ribs, another bolt of pain rifling through me.

None of this seems strange, though. In fact, it seems like I've been waiting for it all my life. The strange part is this: Part of me *appreciates* the pain, like it completes something that was missing a piece.

After two more kicks he just stands over me, one foot on the floor, another on my throat. He toys with the pressure on my throat, rocking forward a bit and then easing off.

Before he lets me go, he laughs—just a small little chuckle finding its way out of him. When he walks to fetch another beer, I pull myself off the floor, every inch of me aching, and leave, the rain coming down so hard on my face it stings.

* * *

I've been outside his house so many times. With the rain still pouring, soaking me through my clothes and bouncing off the handlebars of my bike, I stare into Wilson's house. Inside, I can see people moving, mingling, shadows talking to each other, raising glasses, laughing. I see silhouettes of girls and I think in the middle of them I can distinguish Wilson.

It looks cozy inside. Out here, despite the storm, the night still holds a heat, like if the rain stopped I would go right back to sweating. My head and ribs pulse with pain every time I breathe, and I feel swollen all over.

I can't go in, I know. Not that Wilson doesn't want me, but because I don't want all those eyes turning on me—making an appearance, drenched and bleeding, half the eyes already knowing that I'm the one behind Lindy coming back to town, the force behind Roverson leaving.

All this time, I've wanted some identity, to be able to be noticed by the people who are drawn to Wilson. They'd notice me now, I suppose, but it's not what I had in mind.

I retrace the whole thing in my mind. I think about that night at the start of summer, Wilson and me creeping through the field toward Roverson's, everything full of potential. How did it end up like this?

I pedal up the street, thinking about all of it, fighting off the urge to just ride as far as I can from town—the urge that Roverson gave in to. I retrace the summer in my head, from the moment Wilson and I first lifted that Lincoln for a joyride, but I can't pinpoint the moment that changed everything, that started me irretrievably to now. And maybe there isn't one. Maybe this was in store for me, Roverson or not. But that—blaming it on fate—just seems too convenient.

I turn around and head down the slick pavement to look into Wilson's house again. I realize for the first time just how much I've wrecked, what exactly I've done—to Lindy, to Roverson, to Wilson, to myself. And to Lauryn. All these horrible things I've done to Lauryn, and she's the only one who doesn't hate me for it. The only one who allows me to hope that there's still something more left for me, a future—a tainted, difficult future, but a future nonetheless. Now that I've ruined everything, all I can do is start rebuilding my life—there's nothing left to tear down.

The rain slows now and then, letting sounds of the party reach me. Laughter, music, shouts. It could have all been different, I think. Maybe it still can be different. I have to believe that.

Across the street, I see Wilson's front door open. I squint through the rain and see that it's Wilson himself, cigarette in hand. He leans against the jamb of his door, and looks in my direction. In the storm, I don't know if he can recognize me or not.

He starts to raise his hand, as if he's going to motion me in, but it stops midway and then just lifts the cigarette to his lips.

Maybe there's still time for me to go in, clean up, and join the party. Or maybe I just wanted this—one more glimpse of my friend before he's gone forever.

Either way, it is my choice. Mine.

YOU ARE HERE